THE BRIDE OF FRANKENSTEIN

BearManor Media
P.O. Box 1129
Duncan, OK 73534-1129

Phone: 580-252-3547
Fax: 814-690-1559

www.bearmanormedia.com

The Bride of Frankenstein by Michael Egremont first published:
Queensway Books, London,1935

First USA printing by BOOKFINGER, 1976 (Limited edition)

First BearManor Media Edition 2012

The Nightmares Series is being published to preserve original movie
tie-in novels that were printed in the 1950's and 1960's on the old style pulp
paper. We hope these reprints will allow them to last into the new century.

Philip J. Riley's
NIGHTMARE SERIES

The Brides of Dracula
The Revenge of Frankenstein
The Raven

THE BRIDE OF FRANKENSTEIN

By
Michael Egremont

Philip J. Riley's

NIGHTMARE SERIES

BearManor Media

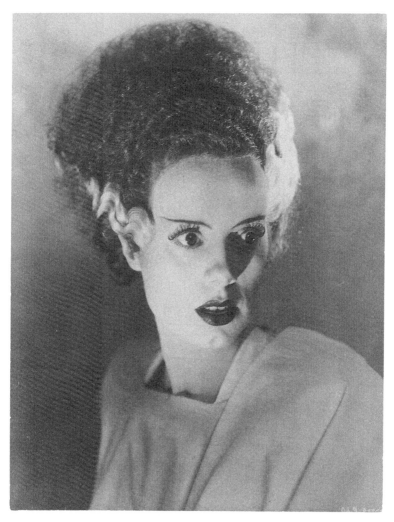

Elsa Lanchester, who portrayed "The Bride" in the Universal Picture

THE BRIDE OF FRANKENSTEIN

PROLOGUE

FOR hours the storm had raged without abatement. Within that long, gracious room, it was warm and comfortable; yet the howling of the wind, and the rain driving furiously against the tall windows, seemed to destroy much of the quiet peace which was the room's usual most notice-able quality.

By one of the french windows, across which the curtains had not yet been drawn, stood a young man, gazing out at the wild night. On his pale, handsome face was a look that might have been interpreted as a certain cynical amusement, which again might have been not unconnected with the young woman, whose curly ringlets were now dropping over the em-broidery frame she held on her lap.

It would not have been surprising that a smile of cynical amusement should have hovered on the delicately chiselled brow of the handsome young man; for that face, striking in its perfect Grecian beauty, belonged to one who was at once the most famous and most notorious of his day.

"I awoke," he said once. "to find myself famous," but his notoriety cannot have come to him in so surprisingly sudden a manner, for he had worked assiduously to earn it.

Yet even the most retiring country miss might have been thrilled (in spite of his reputation) to have entered that room, and recognized the pale, refined features, instead of marring, the beauty of George Gordon-Lord Byron.

Had her mother been there, she might have remarked with a disap-proving sniff, that my lord was in a company not unsuited to his taste and reputation, but hardly . . . well, hardly, the place for *respectable* people. Not indeed that Percy Bysshe Shelley, the young poet, was not respectable by our standards; but in those days, people took a different view of those who set up to criticize existing laws and customs; and the undergraduate who wrote as a practical joke, "A Defence of Atheism," was promptly (and most people thought very reasonable) sent down from his college.

Of Mary, his wife, whose industrious embroidering had just provoked the gentle mockery of Lord Byron's smile, it could hardly be said that she justly shared the curious reputation of her husband and his friend. Yet she was the daughter of that famous Mary Wollstonecraft who had so shocked the England of the late eighteenth century with her outspoken views of revolution, free love, and votes for women! So that when her daughter, taking too seriously the teaching of her philosopher father, William Godwin, decided that a revolutionary young poet would make an excellent husband, England shook its head, and murmured that heredity counted for a lot.

From her needlework, she said.

"The storm seems to interest you Lord Byron?"

He smiled down at her, as he answered, mocking his own mood, "Yes . . . how beautifully romantic! The crudest, savage exhibition of Nature at her worst without: and we three, we elegant three, within . . . ! I should like," he added, smiling, "to think that an irate Jehovah was pointing those arrows of lightning directly at my head. . . ."

"Lord Byron!"

"Yes," he continued, " at the unbowed head of George Gordon, Lord Byron—England's greatest sinner!"

Shelley looked up form the manuscript which he had been correcting. The young nobleman caught the amused look on his friend's face. He waved a deprecating hand.

"But I cannot flatter myself to that extent. Possibly the thunders are for our dear Shelley: Heaven's applause for England's greatest poet."

Now, that last remark might have been the cause of a little misunderstanding, although posterity was to confirm what Shelley already knew in his own mind, that fate had selected him for immortality, while the fame of the handsome Byron was destined to be an evanescent thing; the fashion of a few years, based as it was, on the less enduring appeal to the taste of a moment.

Shelley accepted the compliment, knowing well what name was conjured up in his friend's mind by the words "England's greatest poet." But the truly great are never in doubt of their greatness. That is why they can afford to wait: why they can stand aside and let lesser men pant and strive for the limelight of an hour, knowing, beyond the possibility of a peradventure, that theirs is the sunlight of eternity.

So with that ready tact which even a revolutionary poet can on occasion command, he merely shook his head, and asked quietly:

"What of my Mary?"

Said George Byron, with that charming smile which had made such havoc in the ranks of his enemies:

"She is an angel!"

"Of course," he said. "Mary, you hear the storm: come and watch it with me."

She shook her head in a quick, nervous gesture.

"Oh, no, no! You know how lightning alarms me!"

She turned to her husband, ignoring Lord Byron's smile. "Shelley, darling, will you please light these candles for me?"

Percy Shelley laughed.

"Oh, Mary darling. . . !"

And Byron said, shrugging his shoulders at the incomprehensible ways of women (though indeed he was credited with knowing more about their ways than was good for him);

"Astonishing creature!"

Mary frowned in puzzlement.

"I, Lord Byron?"

He bowed ironically.

"You, my dear young lady! Frightened of thunder; fearful of the dark. . . ."

He fixed his large eyes on her with impudent raillery, while she returned his glance with a half-defiant stare.

"Well. . . ?"

"And yet," he continued, in the same mocking tone, "you have written a tale that sent my blood into icy creeps."

The young authoress laughed contentedly at the compliment, smilingly though it was made; and Byron, turning to where Shelley stood before the blazing fire, asked:

"Can you believe that that bland and lovely brow conceived a Frankenstein—a monster created from the corpses taken from rifled graves. . . . Isn't it astonishing!"

Mary said: "I don't know why you should think so. . . ."

"No . . . ?"

"Well," shrugging her shoulders, and smiling at the two men, "such an audience needs something a little stronger than a pretty little love story."

"Well!"

"So why shouldn't I write of monsters?"

"Rather an ambiguous remark, George? her husband said.

Byron nodded. "It is rather," he said. "No wonder Murray has refused to publish the book. He says their reading public would be too shocked."

Mary looked up from her needlework, to say quietly:

"It will be published, I think."

Shelley sat down, and picked up his manuscript once more. He said, shaking his head:

"Then, darling, you'll have much to answer for."

Mary smiled, and looking up, saw a sympathetic twinkle in Lord Byron's grey eyes. Then, grown suddenly serious, she said:

"I suppose none of us . . . artists—(may I call myself an artist, Percy?)— none of us artists, then, ever write anything that is understood exactly as we meant it to be read. Is that so, Lord Byron?"

He nodded gravely, and she continued:"I don't need to ask Percy: I know how misunderstood has been everything that he has ever written: how twisted and turned every line, until even *he* had to think to remember what he had originally intended. And it was the same with poor Mr. Keats I know."

She smiled, as if to apologize for her little outburst.

"I meant to say," she explained, "that with me, as with others, there was a misunderstanding. The publishers did not see that my purpose was to write a moral lesson—to show in other words, the punishment that befell a mortal man who dared to emulate God."

"Well," said Byron, "whatever your purpose my have been, my dear, I myself take great relish in savouring each separate horror. I roll them," he said, with unctuous relish, "over on my tongue. . . ."

A small white hand clenched against her breast. Mary implored:

"Don't, don't, Lord Byron! . . . Don't remind me of it to-night!"

"What a setting in that churchyard. . . . Can't you see it? First of all, the sobbing women following the priest up the hill to the moonlit cemetery. Then the priest up on the hill to the moonlit cemetery. Then the dull sound of the earth falling on the coffin. . . that was a pretty chill! Then Frankenstein and the dwarf stealing the body out of its newly-made grave. . . ."

He shook his head in wonder.

"How does she think of these gruesome things, Percy? I really don't know. . . where were we? Oh yes! Then they cut the hanged man down from the gallows, where he swung creaking in the wind. . . ."

The french windows rattled, and around the house the gale howled and moaned.

"Exactly," he smiled, " as it is howling to-night."

But Mary, bent over her embroidery, did not see his smile. Instead, he could see the picture that Lord Byron was painting with such clarity: the dark mountain abode of Henry Frankenstein, lit only by the thin, wan light of a watery moon: the shadow-swamped castle where taking dead men apart, he built up a human monster.

Lord Byron's voice broke in on his vivid dreaming.

"So fearful, so horrible," he was saying, "that only a half-crazed brain could have devised such a travesty of nature. And them, at last, Frankenstein himself thrown from the top of the burning mill by the very monster he created."

Mary looked up with shining eyes.

"Yes," she cried eagerly. "That's what I meant just now. *That* was retribution."

The young *beau* smiled at her agitation. Ignoring her pleading, he continued:

"Yes," he said, "retribution, if you like. But oh, what a nightmare! And to think," he smiled, "that it was these fragile white fingers that penned the nightmare!" She gave a little cry that brought her husband hurrying across to her.

"Darling, what is it?"

"Oh nothing, really. Only that Lord Byron distracted me, and made me prick myself. Look, it's bleeding!"

With gentle care her husband wrapped his handkerchief about her fingers.

"There, there. Does it hurt?"

She shook her head, smiling at his tender solicitude.

"Not much, dear."

He said: "I do think a shame, Mary, that your story ended quite suddenly . . . I, for one, would have liked to know what happened after Frankenstein's body went crashing down from the roof of the mill. . . ."

"Well," said Mary quietly, "It so happens that that wasn't the end of all."

"No!"

"Yes," smiling. "Would you like to hear what happened after that?"

The two men drew their chairs closer, one on each side of her.

She said: "Do you know, I feel like telling it. After all, it's a perfect night for mystery and horror—the air itself is filled with monsters."

Byron laughed. "I am all ears! While Heaven blasts the night without, open up your pits of hell!"

The room seemed suddenly to drop into silence, as the two young men waited for Mary to begin.

She said, quietly: "Well, then, imagine yourselves standing by the wreckage of the mill. The fire has died down, and only the bare skeleton of the building is visible; the gaunt rafters stark against the sky. . . ."

CHAPTER I

THE HOMECOMING

IT was now some hours since the body of the young Baron Henry Frankenstein had been carried to his castle, on its last sorrowful journey; but around the still blazing skeleton of the mill, a crowd was yet gathered; the aftermath of onlookers, who have come to enjoy, as it were, the shadow of a thrill; to quicken, not at seeing, so much, as at what has been seen of others.

Minnie, though, was not of these. She was a privileged spectator; not only from the fact that she had been one of the first at the fire, but because, as the Baroness Elizabeth's maid, she had (no one would deny it) an enviable connection with the principal character of this curious affair.

Marta, her companion, was silent; awed by the leaping tongues of fire; the successive crashes as vanes and sail and superstructure went hurtling down into the stream that ran beside the mill. Besides, the dramatic implication of the tragedy was not lost upon her. She had seen, for one shocked second, the white agonized face of the young Baron, as the gentle hands of the townsfolk and villagers (many of whom were his own tenants) had lifted him in silent grief on to a stretcher, hastily improvised from staves and jackets.

But even a fire which had destroyed the finest mill in the Duchy, to say nothing of the lives of a man, and the monster his wayward genius had created from the plunder of rifled graves, could still Minnie's tongue.

"Well, she said, with unmistaken gratification, as the whole cowling collapsed into the brick lower-course of the building, "I must say that's the best fire I ever say in all my life!"

Marta blinked at her through her tears, a little shocked at her companion's short laugh.

"Minnie!"

"What is it?"

"Well," shrugging her shoulders; "after all. . . ."

Marta was not good at explanations; but Minnie was not so easily put off.

"After all . . . What?" she asked shaking the sobbing girl. "What *are* you crying for?" "Oh, Minnie . . . it's terrible!" Marta said.

"I know it's terrible; but after all them murders, and now poor Baron Henry being brought home to die, well, can't you understand that I'm glad to see the monster roasted before my very eyes. Death," she added vindictively, "is too good for him."

She shuddered, crossing herself; suddenly sobered at the recollection of those terror-haunted days, which had come to an end, only with the events of this tragic night.

She muttered, half to herself:

"It's all the devils' work; and you'd better cross yourself quick, Marta, before he gets you!"

A voice was raised behind them; a harsh, dictatorial voice; that of a man who tries to cover a congenital absence of any intrinsic authority by the affectation of a bullying manner. It was the Burgomaster, endeavouring to restore that prestige which had suffered in the last few weeks such lamentable damage, when his martinet ways had failed most signally to prevent the murders of women and children at the hands of the Monster.

But he was not above trying:

"Now, come along!" he was shouting, above the hubbub of the crowd. "Come along; it's all over." And as no move was made to obey his injunction, he added, "Go back to your homes, and go to sleep!"

Yet, as he realized with a sinking heart, there was more to see: and he knew, to, how vain was that hope that the crowd might be persuaded to disperse before every splinter of that mill was charcoal: every spark cold.

There was an excited scream from Minnie, which caused the Burgomaster to glance frowning in her direction: he had already suffered from the maid's sharp tongue. He heard her say.

"There it goes again! It ain't burned out at all: there's more yet!"

And Marta's simple question:

"What! Isn't the Monster dead yet?"

He moved into the crowd, waving his silver-headed cane, with very much the same gesture as a shepherd employs to manœuvre his flock. "Come *along*," he pleaded, with wistful impatience. "It's time every decent man and woman was in bed."

There was a sudden spurt of flame, and he heard Minnie's voice:

"His insides caught at last: insides is always the last to be consumed."

"Move on," said the Burgomaster, "you've had enough excitement for one night." And as they seemed reluctant to go: "This strange man you called the Monster is *dead!*" He added, "Monster indeed . . . ! You can thank your lucky stars they sent for me to safeguard life and property."

He glanced nervously in the direction of Minnie: she was not looking at him, and he could see the profile of her angular face, lined against the darkness by the light of the fire. He was mistaken, though, in thinking that the remark had gone unnoticed.

She turned towards him, to say bitterly:

"Why didn't you safeguard them as lies drowned and murdered?"

The authority of law is always invoked when man's authority fails: a poor substitute, but better than none.

It was invoked now, by the Burgomaster. He blew out his cheeks to hide his embarrassment, and uttered the familiar cry:

"Come now! I want no rioting! No riots, now!"

Said Minnie contemptuously; "Who's rioting?"

(Ah that woman!) Quite patiently, considering everything, the Chief Citizen sighed:

"Move on, move on, *please.* Good night all . . . and pleasant dreams!"

A voice said:

"Ah! pleasant dreams yourself! Everybody: just because he's the Burgomaster: hoot!"

Not a nice woman, by any means. . . .

But the crowd had begun to disperse; and the flames of the mill had died low. Minnie walked over to where a knot of silent people stood around the bier on which Baron Henry's still body lay.

"Poor Baron Henry," a woman said, weeping, "he was to have been married to-day to that lovely girl, Elizabeth."

"Cover him up," said the Burgomaster. "come, woman, we must break the news to the poor girl."

He turned to a man who was holding a horse by its bridle.

"Here you, ride as fast as you can to the Castle, and tell the old Baron Frankenstein that we are bringing his son home."

The man rode off, and as he did so, the flames of the burning mill expired in one last glittering tongue of fire, which lit up the flying figure of the horseman and the wan faces of the crowd,

The sob of a woman broke the heavy silence.

The crowd turned homewards, leaving but half a dozen of their company to carry the bier. Sleep called them. The act was played: the curtain had fallen at last on the strangest drama of all.

CHAPTER II

"HE *must* BE DEAD. . . ."

Long after the little procession had wound its way up the rocky path to the grim Schloss Frankenstein, a man and woman stood in argument on the deserted hill. Above them, towered the blackened ruins of the mill; around them, was only the silence of the night.

It was obvious that their argument was deep: that the man was obstinate, and the woman fearful. She was holding his arm as if to restrain him from some impetuous and foolish act; and from the surly efforts he made to free himself from her grasp, it was equally obvious that his mind was set on a course from which her pleadings would serve little to deflect him.

"Come now, Hans," she was saying, "the Monster is dead now. Nothing could be left alive in that furnace. Why," she asked him, weeping, "do you stay here?"

Doggedly: "I want to see with my own eyes. . . ."

"Ah, but Hans! He *must* be dead . . ." she whimpered: it was cold, and the dark silence was oppressive: frightening. "Besides," she added. "whether he's dead or alive, nothing can bring our little Maria back to us."

She fixed her wide eyes on her husband's dark, set face. He shook his head, a little ashamed of his obstinacy (for he was not altogether indifferent to her pleading; not unaware that in some matters women have an intuition that transcends knowledge: that "thoughts go blowing through them, wiser than their own"). But for all that, some dogged purpose, the blind unthinking purpose of the peasant drove him on.

He muttered, averting his gaze from where her face showed a white patch in the thin moonlight.

"If I see his blackened bones, I can sleep at night."

As he spoke, he turned on his heel, trying to shake off his wife's restraining arm. He made his slow way up the hill, towards the black bulk of the ruined mill.

"Hans! come back. . . ."

He shook his head at that frantic cry: forcing his way forward, against the frantic reproaches and adjurations that followed him. At last they stood beside the mill; Hans poking at the still smouldering wood with his long stick. There was a brick stairway leading to what was once the door. It was still, apparently, sound; and Hans went up, poking with his stick.

From the ground his wife watched him, with fear and despair in her heart.

"Hans," she whispered, "you'll be burnt yourself. . . . Ah!" she beat her bosom with a clenched fist, whose knuckles gleamed white in the light of the moon. "Maria drowned to death, and you burned up. . . . What," she murmured brokenly, "shall I do then?"

And as if in those wild words there had been something of a prophecy, there came a sound to shatter the stillness, and send her running up the blackened steps. It was a gasp, a cry. And the cry came from her husband, as the charred flooring of the mill gave way, and he plunged down into the cistern beneath. . . .

There was nothing to see as Hans' wife bent over the dark pit that lay beneath. Only to her frightened ears came the agitated splashing, the hurried gasps that told her where her husband was struggling beneath.

A thin ray of moonlight, piercing a hole in the ruined wall, lit up a corner of the pool, but where the radiance fell, there was no movement.

But the splashing continued, and the woman stood back a little, looking for a rope, or some instrument by which she might render assistance.

It was curious that she should have chosen that moment to search, for she glanced below, at that spot where the cold light rippled on the darkly stirring waters, she might have seen that which froze the blood in her husband's veins and strangled the cry that rose to his lips.

For out of the darkness came an arm and a hand: moving with a sinister, *inhuman* slowness above the surface of the water.

Hans could not cry out: he opened his mouth to scream: but a dry whisper that did not rise above the splashing of his wild arms, was all that he could utter, in a madness of terror, his flailing arms beat at the cold stagnant waters: the only thought in his crazed mind was of escape.

But eyes which had once seen the darkness of death, pierced the half-gloom of that dank pit. Following the frantic man came another shape, which moved with a slow, terrifying purposefulness; which seemed too sure even to hurry; and which, cornering the helpless Hans as a cat corners a mouse, dragged him snarling under water. . . .

There was a ladder leading from the cistern to the main chamber of the mill, and by the head of this ladder stood Hans' wife. She had discovered no rope by which she could assist him to rise, but the continuous splashing had allayed her fears somewhat. The noise assured her that her husband was not drowned. Only, she wondered a little why he did not call to her. . . .

At last she said: "Hans, where are you? Hans, are you all right?"

In the darkness below something stirred; and at the foot of the ladder, she saw the drops of water glisten as a figure rose to view. She heard the sound of feet on the ladder.

She sighed in relief.

"I hear you Hans. Here. . . ."

"This will teach him." she muttered; not altogether displeased that her husband's obstinacy had earned him a soaking.

Her hand was grasped, and step by step the ladder was ascended. The man, still grasping her hand, climbed up on to the floor. The moonlight fell full on the dripping figure and the domed head. The scarred white face was to terribly familiar, that Hans' wife should not have screamed. Screamed once, in an agony of horror and despair.

Once she screamed, and once only. It was the last time she ever did so; for she was still screaming as two strong hands picked her up; and holding her poised for one second above the gaping maw of the cistern, cast her down into the oily waters below.

After that there was a silence, broken only by the hooting of an owl. . . .

CHAPTER III

THE RETURN

NOW Minnie retained her position at the Castle because of two reasons: that she was an efficient and willing servant; and that both her mother and her grandmother had been in the service of the Frankenstein family.

It was as well that she enjoyed these two excellent recommendations; for surely, had her pedigree been shorter, or her duties less meticulously discharged, she had long since paid the price of her unappeasable curiosity and ungovernable tongue.

One would have thought that with the taking of Baron Henry's body up to the Castle, the affair of the Monster might have been considered closed. Actually it was, to every other inhabitant of the Duchy (or so they thought), but Minnie, as I have said, had a curiosity that was truly unappeasable: it was more that; it was the dominating passion of her life.

Had she been born in other surroundings, had she been given by Fate to play a greater part than was accorded her, she might have gone down to History as one of the great investigators of the world: have been classed with those great names, whose lust for forbidden knowledge has entered into the proverbial wisdom of the world: she might have been of that glamorous company whereof are Actæon, and Peeping Tom of Coventry; Pandora, and Lot's wife. . . .

But these speculations are idle. She was, in fact, nothing more than an extremely inquisitive person, whose curiosity had never been in the least degree repressed.

One can quite understand, then, why she left the procession half-way on its journey up the mountain path to the Castle, and hurried back the way she had come. As she explained to herself: "For one last look."

It was, by an irony of fate, the first look. Of all those people who shivered through the breathless weeks that followed the return of the Monster who survived that nerve-racking ordeal; she was the first to cast eyes on his miraculous resurrected body . . . and live.

She was not observing much where she was going; being more engrossed in avoiding the potholes and hummocks, than seeing what lay ahead. It was simply some sixth sense which caused her to look up, just as she was about to collide with a dark shape that towered above her; whose head was lined so strangely high and square against the waning moon.

But she stopped in time, halting for one stricken second to gaze upon that terrifying figure that she knew only too well.

Then, with a wild scream, she turned and ran headlong down the hill, her shawl dropping from her unheeded; while, with shriek after shriek, she shattered the elemental silence of the night.

CHAPTER IV

AT CASTLE FRANKENSTEIN. A STRANGE AWAKENING

THE ancient castle of Frankenstein was one of those grim, towering mediæval fortresses that one only sees in Germany and Bohemia—many-turretted structures of so bizarre a design that they seem to belong to the fantastic illustrations of Gustave Doré, and never to a world of reality.

So it is, that the sight of them always conjures up a long-forgotten world, of ancient sins and vanished loves; but which yet shroud the grey stones of pinnacle and battlement in a sort of mist of remembrance.

Even on sunny days, the arched gate of the Keep is always in shadow: pools of shade lie beyond the portcullis gate; and from below it is hard to imagine that life, let alone young hopes and young laughter could exist within the cold, dead spaces of the narrow windows.

It was perched on a high crag which overlooked the little river: the well-guarded pathway wound up that side of the hill which faced the town: the other side ran precipitously down to the river below: an almost vertical face of rock, rising a sheer eight hundred feet and offering foothold neither to man nor beast. Schloss Frankenstein had been built in days when the saying "Every man's home is his castle" had a meaning of deep significance. They were wild days, when outlaws and robber bands roamed the valley of the Rhine; when life was cheap, and might the only right.

Yet architects who had built Frankenstein, had known their art. For several hundred years the grim pile had dominated the country around; aloof, impregnable, watching with cold, unemotional regard, the passing of faiths and kingdoms; hearing from afar off the crash of the fall of tyrants and saviours.

So much for its external appearance. The interior was in keeping with the gloomy fantasy of the outside; bare stone walls, with groined ceilings supported by squat columns, in the carved foliage of whose capitals lurked the grotesque monsters of monkish fancy and dark superstition. From the frescoed walls, the dim figures of the long-fingered saints, stared wide-eyed, while they trod airily with their splay feet, upon leering, recumbent devils, that seemed more at home in Frankenstein's gloomy hall than they.

The furnishings of the Castle, though naturally newer than its decorations, yet seemed to partake of the sense of incredible age with which the whole place was informed. Old Gothic chairs, with high carved back, looking like the thrones of mediæval kings; low Italian chairs, shaped like hour glasses, covered with faded ruby velvet; chairs and tables from the ateliers of Marot and Buhl, on which the gilt had long since faded to show the red beneath; or the brass so cunningly inlaid by King Louis's master craftsman, parted years ago from the carefully fretted tortoiseshell. No matter what was there, however many centuries separated the makers of these things; in Frankenstein, all things were the same. Over everything, like a pall hung the curious, paradoxical sense of something that was at once everlasting and decaying: a moribund something that yet endure to the end of all things.

That was how it had always seemed to Elizabeth. Ever since she had come to stay with her uncle, the old Baron Frankenstein, she had had that sense of an innate enmity in the gloomy surroundings of the Castle: as though the old stones resented her presence there; thought of her as an interloper; and were watching and waiting their time, until their ancient strength might be manifest, and she expelled into that alien world from which she had come to intrude upon their brooding peace.

She had never before admitted to herself that she was unhappy in Frankenstein; much less admit that she loathed and feared the place, with an intensity which caused her to wonder that she had the capacity for such deep emotion. Before the terrifying events of the last few weeks had driven her into examining her own mind and feelings, she had always shrugged away the uneasy fancies which beset her, as she wandered through the gloomy chambers and corridors of the ancient Castle. And, besides, if, deep down in her heart, she did admit that the heavy architecture and outworn decorations weighed heavily on her spirit, she had consoled herself in the thought that when one day she should be the châtelaine of Frankenstein, she might do some thing to introduce a little brightness into that bleak, comfortless abode.

And this day had been almost more than she could bear. Henry was away, God knew where; and from the town, from the hints dropped by the servants, Elizabeth had learnt vaguely of the terror-stricken nights which had culminated in the desperate manhunt, and finally, the burning of the mill.

That last she had watched herself, from the balcony overlooking the drawbridge, and thus, directly facing the town. She had seen the flames mount higher and higher, until the hill crowned with the mill had seemed like some monstrous volcano erupting in the night. From afar she had heard the hubbub of the crowd, seen the dancing specks of light that were lanterns, almost blotted out by the fire's fierce glare.

Then, when the fire had almost died, a scream came to her on the night air; a cry of alarm; and terror; and horror; as though the crowd had witnessed some happening of more than ordinary fearfulness. She had wondered what it had been; but there was no one near who could have told her. Everyone seemed to have deserted her; Minnie was gone; and only the butler was dozing in his hooded seat within the main door.

Suddenly she realized that she was shivering. She pulled her cashmere shawl more tightly around her shoulders as she stared out at where the burnt mill now showed, a black shape against the risen moon. Over everything had come a silence that was almost palpable: there were no voices, and the stillness was a thing to make one marvel.

Again she shivered, and this time she knew that it was not altogether that the night was cold.

She turned, and went through the open french window into her room.

As Elizabeth had re-entered the house, trembling, as two horsemen had clatter across the drawbridge; and before she had turned back into her room, the girl had seen servants and retainers (sprung apparently from nowhere) crowd around the men.

Full of a dreadful foreboding, Elizabeth laid aside her shawl, and straightening her hair at a little Italian mirror which hung beside the door, went out of the room, and walked slowly down the stairs. Had she found the courage, she would have run back to her bedroom, and hidden her face, sobbing in the pillows; for these weeks of alarm and fears had sapped almost all her reserve of strength. Yet she knew that her duty lay below: that people were looking to her, the Baroness Frankenstein, to comport herself with that dignity, which however it might lack in them, would be demanded of her.

What lay below she knew not; yet of this one thing she was certain, that these messengers were messengers of ill-tidings. As she came to the bottom of the stairs, she rook a deep breath, squared her shoulders, and prepared herself to face the worst. It was not long in arriving, for, as she came around the corner of the staircase, she saw the butler open the doors, flinging them wide; to disclose such a scene as made her heart for an instant cease its beating.

In the great courtyard of the castle, men were standing about a wagon; men with flaming torches, and pale, anxious looks. Even from within the doorway, Elizabeth could see the anxiety on their rugged, open faces: anxiety, and a certain nameless quality of tenderness, of pity. . . .

The butler stood aside as she came up, to stand framed in the mighty portal, with the light streaming out behind her, and throwing her shadow across rough cobbles of the castle courtyard. No one stirred, or spoke. But every eye was upon her as she stood there, comprehensions slowly welling up within her brain, bringing with it a sickening, choking terror that could not be shaken off.

Among all those silent, watchful people, she had, suddenly, the feeling of an animal, hemmed in, trapped . . . faced with something worse than death.

She shook herself. This would not do. Something was expected of her: a duty that must transcend all petty considerations of self.

There was a leader among these people: a tall, fair peasant dressed in the green velvet of a woodsman. To him Elizabeth addressed herself.

Quietly she asked, "Henry. . . . is he killed?"

The man shrank from her bright gaze, crossing himself as he answered.

"Oh, my lady," he murmured, "how can we tell you?"

Wildly Elizabeth looked around her. Some of the women were weeping; and the heads of the men were bared.

Then, for the first time, she saw what they had brought with them. By the steps, two men were standing, bearing a stretcher, on which, covered with a white cloth, was a figure, whose ominous stillness brought a cry to the girl's lips.

The men were about to enter the castle, as the cry halted them. They stood still: while Elizabeth, raising the sheet, gazed on the pale, drawn features of her betrothed.

For a heavy minute she stood gazing down at him, lost in memory.

Then quietly, she signalled the two men to follow her, as she went up the steps into the Castle.

In the meantime, another visitor had come across the drawbridge and entered the courtyard, just as the bier was being carried into the Castle. But this visitor was running, and her loose hair and heaving bosom seemed to indicate that she had been running for some considerable time; while from her pale face and trembling hands, one could infer that the news she brought was not altogether good.

It was Minnie; and although the procession had had nearly half an hour's start of her, she had caught it up.

The butler said suspiciously,, "Where have *you* come from? The Baroness was wondering where you'd got to!"

Minnie clutched his arm, almost incoherent from terror.

"It's out again, Albert!"

He removed the restraining arm with the dignity of his tribe.

"What," he asked coldly, "do you want? Been drinking again?"

She was to terrified to take exception to this remark. People had begun to gather round, curious to know what the maid was saying. She was whimpering now.

"It's alive! The Monster, Albert! It's alive. . . !"

A peasant sniggered, and winking at the butler, made a gesture of raising a glass to his mouth. The butler nodded.

"Ah, be quiet, you old fool!"

"But," she pleaded, "I *saw* it! It ain't turned to no skeleton at all! It lived right through the fire!"

The butler turned on the step.

"Ah," he said, sneering, "go bite your tongue off! We don't believe in ghosts here!"

"All right," she murmured, "I wash my hands of it. Nobody will believe me. Very well; let 'em be murdered in their beds, for all *I* care . . . Pah!"

She came up the steps behind Albert, peering inquisitively at the knot of people, maids, and men servants mostly, who were standing with Elizabeth around the long table in the hall. Terror had not killed Minnie's curiosity; and soon she had elbowed her way though the crowd, until she stood by the table, gazing down at the dead body of the Baron Henry.

Minnie said, in a hushed whisper, "Oh my lady, he'll never speak again. . . ."

Elizabeth shook her head, as one who dreams, and whose dreams are ill.

"I was foretold of this," she murmured. "I was told to beware of my wedding night."

The sob of a woman broke the stillness of that great room.

"Come, my lady," said another, taking Elizabeth's limp hand, and leading her unprotesting away.

It was as well that Elizabeth had gone; that she should have heard Minnie's scream rather than seen that which had inspired it. She was half way up the staircase, as that strident shriek shattered the heavy silence, and brought her running back to where Henry's body was lying.

For Minnie had screamed, "Oh, look! My lady! He's alive! He's *alive!*"

As Elizabeth came up she saw the terrified maid shrink back from a feebly moving arm; while the ring of servants drew away, crossing themselves in superstitious fear. So Elizabeth seemed quite alone, as she bent sobbing over her lover, moaning softly.

"Oh Henry! . . . Henry darling!"

She kissed his cold, pale forehead, and the eyes opened. For a long moment they stared at her uncomprehending. Then, at last, understanding wakened, and they lit up with a wan smile.

"Elizabeth!"

The girl turned and beckoned to two of the men to carry the stretcher upstairs.

CHAPTER V

THE SHADOWS BETWEEN

ELIZABETH, her hand smoothing Henry's hair, as he sat, propped up in the great four-poster bed, said to the maid, "You can go to bed now, Mary."

The girl, put the tray she was carrying, down before the fireplace, and went out of the room.

As the door closed behind her, Elizabeth bent down and kissed Henry on the cheek. Her eyes were radiant with happiness, and looking up at her, Henry knew a sudden warm comfort in the thought of her love.

"Sit down here."

He patted the bed, and she sat on its side, watching him, with anxious, loving regard.

"You'll soon be better, Henry."

He smiled, taking her hand in his, and pressing it to his lips.

"I feel almost myself again."

She nodded.

"As soon as you're strong enough, we'll go away—and we'll forget all this horrible experience."

He shuddered, "Forget. . . !"

A cold wind seemed to blow through their hearts as he said it.

"If only I *could* forget! But it's never out of my mind. . . ."

She put an arm around him, comforting him, as she would comfort a child that has awakened screaming from the terror that walks by night.

"I've been cursed," Henry was whispering, "cursed for delving into the mysteries of Life. Perhaps," he said musingly, "Death is sacred . . . and I profaned it. But oh, what a wonderful vision it was!

His eyes lit up as he spoke, blazing with the fanatic visionary look of the scientist, who has not only journeyed to the edge of the beyond, but more, for moments has been permitted to gaze over it. Elizabeth's heart grew cold as she watched him, and over her (unreasonably, as she told herself) swept again that tide of foreboding, which had first come when the gypsy fortune-teller had warned her of impending mischance.

She whispered, "Oh, my dear. . . ." and Henry saw that her eyes were filled with tears,

He patted her hand, smiling, as one might smile at the fears of a child. "My dear, why are you worrying. . . ?"

She shook her head: a tired, bewildered gesture.

"Oh . . . I don't know . . . I'm so frightened, Henry!"

He said, "You needn't be . . . What has happened is past; is done with. . . The future is ours and ours, alone. . . ."

"And God's Henry," she reminded him, gently.

"Yes," he murmured . . . "and God's . . . Yet," he continued, "the vision was wonderful. I dreamed of being the first to give to the world the secret that God is so jealous of; the formula for Life. Ah! think of the power to create a man!" he said eagerly, "and I did, Elizabeth . . . I did it! I created a man! And who knows," he whispered, "in time, I might have trained him to my will; found him a soul as well as a body. I might have bred a race . . . ." His voice dropped so low that she could hardly catch the words; and lost in his dreaming, he seemed scarcely to realize that she was there with him. "I might even have found the secret of eternal life. . . !"

"Oh, Henry!" the girl implored, "don't say those things! Don't think them! It's blasphemous and wicked! There are some things we are never meant to know. Surely you see that?"

Her lovely grey eyes were filled with such pathetic appeal, that Henry shook his head, sighing— "It may be," he explained, gently, that I'm *intended* to know the secret of Life. It may be part of the Divine plan, Elizabeth!"

She said indignantly, "No, no! It's the Devil, not God, who prompts you! It's Death and not Life, that's in it all, and at the end of it all."

Suddenly firm in decision, she spoke what was in her heart: what indeed she had been intending to tell him ever since she had realized that a miracle had snatched him back from the Valley of the Shadow, and given him back to her.

"Listen, Henry; while you have been lying here, tossing in your delirium, I couldn't sleep. And when you were raving of your insane desire to create living men from the dust of the dead, a strange apparition seemed to appear in this room. It comes—a figure like Death—and each time it appears more clearly—and nearer.

Her breathing was hurried, her bosom heaving. With outstretched forefinger she was pointing to a corner of the room, a place of darkness that lay beyond the soft, weak light of the lamp.

" . . . Nearer, Henry: nearer! It seems to be reaching out for you . . . as if it would take you away from me!"

Frightened at her raving, Henry put his arm around her trembling shoulders.

"Elizabeth, dearest, be quiet. . . ." but she was beyond soothing.

"There it is! Look: there!"

"I see nothing, Elizabeth!" He peered into the dark corner, half apprehensive of her sanity; half fearful that there really were some fearful portent: some vision of evil that the caverns of the night had spewed forth. There were many legends current, concerning the strange things that were sometimes to be seen within the grim walls of Castle Frankenstein; and in its thousand years of history, enough crimes had been committed, and tragedies enacted there, to have peopled every room with ghosts.

But though, with a heart that beat to stifling, he scanned every corner of that long and lofty room, he saw nothing.

"Where is it? he asked her, "There's nothing there."

"There! she screamed, "There! It's coming for you! Nearer! Oh, Henry. . . !"

His arms were tightly around her now, as he sought to quieten her terrified struggles. He was pleading with her to be quiet; but still she moaned; "Henry! Henry! It's here. . .!"

So that at last he drew her down beside him; pressing her shuddering body closely to his, while he kissed her damp forehead, and she laughed hysterically. . . laughed, and laughed, and laughed. . . .

"Elizabeth," he said, "*do* be sensible, dear. . . It's all right: really it is."

She was clinging to him, as a child awakened from nightmare clings to its nurse; and Henry felt a deep warm comfort that she should cling to him.

Then, through the open window, they heard the sound of knocking: of someone thundering on the great doors below.

Michael Egremont

CHAPTER VI

AN UNWELCOME VISITOR AND A CURIOUS REQUEST

IT was, thought Minnie bitterly, as she stepped across the stone floor of the hall, rather hard that Albert had a trick of secreting himself just when he was wanted. And she wondered if this incredible and alarming night would ever end.

The knocking came again; petulant, purposeful knocking, that sent the echoes chasing each other among the shadowy recesses of the groined roof.

"Albert," Minnie murmured fretfully, "where are you? Drat that man! He's never here when he's wanted. What's the good of a stuffed footman anyway!"

Again the knocking, and Minnie's face in the dancing light of the candle she carried, seemed a little anxious, drawn. She was endeavouring to sustain her courage by these peevish apostrophisings; but in reality, as she confessed to herself, it was with the utmost trepidation that she was approaching the front door.

"All right, all right! she snapped, as a sudden sharp tap made her jump, "Don't knock the castle over! We're not all dead yet!"

She put the candlestick down on a small table, while she shot the heavy bolts and turned the ancient key in its creaking lock. Then she opened the door.

It was a tall thin man who stood without; a lean, cadaverous man; with sunken features and glowing eyes; whose long cloak and black slouch-hat did nothing to lessen the effect that his features made on the servant.

She muttered, uncertainly, (mistrusting his look),

"There's nobody at home. . . ."

His thin mouth under the long, sharp nose, twisted in ill-natured mockery.

26

He said impatiently, as though he were addressing a child, "Let me in, my good woman. I *know* the young Baron Frankenstein is at home."

He made no attempt to enter; but his eyes seemed to hold a certainty that no one was likely to cross his will. He had the calm authority of those whose commands are beyond dispute.

Minnie said coldly; "He's sick—he's in his bed—where all decent folk should be at this time of night."

The stranger smiled contemptuously.

"Come," he said, dismissing her angry fear as a thing of no account, "tell him that Doctor Pretorius is here, on a secret matter of grave importance, and must see him alone—to-night." He stressed the last word with an emphasis that Minnie found disturbing.

She backed away from his cold gaze, and walked slowly across the hall to the foot of the stairs. The visitor was following.

She whispered, "What . . . what . . . what was the name?"

"Pretorius," he said, seemingly unaware of her agitation, and as though it were the most usual thing in the world to pay visits in the early dawn.

"Doctor Pretorius."

They went up the stairs together: Minnie bearing the candle, going first; and the Doctor following. Occasionally, the woman would turn, to see, as it were a third shape, that followed them with silent tread: but it was only the candle throwing the shadow of the Doctor's flapping cloak against the panelled walls.

At last they stood outside the door of Henry's bedroom.

"Not, you stay right here," said Minnie, with a shudder at the Doctor's slow, cruel smile.

She knocked; two tiny knocks that sounded absurdly meek. She could *feel* the smile deepen on the face behind her. But the knocks had been heard: for a voice (Elizabeth's it was) asked, "Who's there?"

"It's Minnie, my lady."

"Come in!" It was Henry speaking.

Minnie opened the door and went in, closing it behind her.

"It's Doctor Pretorius," she said. "He says he wants to see the master. Most insistent, he is."

"Pretorius?" Henry frowned.

"Yes," said Minnie, eagerly. "That's the name. He's a very queer-looking gentleman, Sir. And must see you—on a secret, grave matter, he said—to-night—alone."

Elizabeth was looking at Henry as the woman spoke; a look in which curiosity was not unmixed with apprehension. But Henry seemed to know the man.

He said, "Bring him in," and Minnie went across the room to open the door.

Elizabeth's hand sought Henry's and its gentle pressure told that young man more than words could ever have conveyed. It told of undying affection, and undying loyalty, and, if necessary, that fierce love, that age-old maternal instinct, which will make woman a thing of

> 'Ravening Nature,
> Red in tooth and claw. . .'

laying down her life rather than allow her loved one to be harmed. . . .

But now the door had opened, and both heads were turned to see who had entered.

From the doorway Minnie squeaked, "Doctor Pretorius" and vanished.

The tall man advanced, with easy confidence, bowing to Elizabeth, and smiling at Henry. In the lamplight, it could now be seen that he was a man of sixty years of age, but whose erect carriage and insolent air of youthfulness made him appear younger than he really was.

He lisped, with affected nonchalance, "Baron Frankenstein, now I believe?"

Henry said, "Won't you come in, Doctor?"

"Thank you. I trust," the man said evenly, "that you will pardon the intrusion at so late an hour." He coughed. "I should not have ventured to come had I not a communication to make, which, I suspect, may be of the utmost importance to yourself."

Henry said, "Elizabeth, this is Professor Pretorius. He used to be Doctor of Philosophy at the University . . . but . . ."

He broke off in some confusion, and the Doctor laughed.

"My *dear* Baron! Booted is the word. . ." He added with quiet emphasis, "for knowing too much. . ."

He chuckled to himself, glancing with cynical amusement at Elizabeth's white, set face.

"Yes!" he murmured, "just fancy that! For knowing too much. . . ."

Elizabeth said quietly, "Henry's been very ill, Professor. He shouldn't be disturbed."

Her calm gaze was fixed on him as she spoke. But he shrugged his shoulders; and Henry asked:

"Why have you come here, to-night?"

"My business," said Pretorius, "is private, Baron. May I see you alone?"

Elizabeth murmured, "Of course, Henry . . . I shall be within call."

Then, without another word, she walked out of the room.

Not until the door had closed behind Elizabeth, and the sound of her footsteps faded on the polished oak boards of the corridor outside, did Henry ask:

"What do you want?"

The older man was sitting at the foot of the bed, his cloak and hat laid aside. He seemed younger without them, and from him came such an air of purpose and power, that Henry, with a sinking heart, realized that it would take a strong will, indeed, to gainsay this man.

So that, when Pretorius said with his even smile, "We must work together. . . ." Henry shouted:

"This is outrageous! I'm through with it! I'll have no more of this Hell's spawn."

He added, more quietly, "As soon as I'm well, I'm going to be married. . . ."

The mocking voice murmured, "Congratulations. I always think that married life is such an enviable condition . . . for the unmarried."

"Thank you," said Henry curtly, "I don't think, Professor, that I'm interested in your views on marriage."

"A pity: I could have told you such a lot. Well, well . . . now where were we. . . ?"

"I said," Henry snapped, "that as soon as I'm well, I'm going to be married. Then I'm going away."

The professor held up a long white hand in protest.

" My *dear* Baron. I must beg of you to reconsider. . . ."

Henry shook his head, "Never!"

The professor's tone did not change. He shrugged his shoulders, and continued in the same lisping drawl as before, "Yet, you know; do you not? ; it is you, really, who are responsible for all these murders. There are," he explained, "penalties for killing people."

He was watching Henry's face with an intentness that made the young man's heart chill within him.

"With your creature still at large in the countryside. . . ."

His voice was very soft now: soft, with the gentle, purring sibilance of a cat. Nor did his expression alter when Henry asked fiercely:

"Are you threatening me?"

Only his eyebrows hoisted themselves into his pale, lined forehead, as he smiled.

"Don't put it too crudely *please!* I have," he shrugged away the suggestion of any coercion, "I have ventured to hope that you and I together—no longer as master and pupil; but as fellow scientists; might probe together the mysteries of Life and Death."

"Never!" said Henry, shuddering, "no further. . . ."

"And reach," Pretorius continued, as though he had not heard the interruption, "a goal undreamed of by scientists."

Henry wrung his hands in anguish: the sweat beaded on his brow, as he cried:

"Pretorius, you don't understand. Science has nothing to do with it: no claims any more on me. I can't make any further experiments. . . . I've had," he whispered, thinking of the last twenty-four hours, "a terrible lesson. . . ."

The Professor pursed his lips.

"Very sad," he murmured, "very sad! But," he pleaded, "you and I have gone too far, to stop *now*. Nor, indeed," he reflected, "can it be stopped so easily. I have also continued my experiments; and that is why I came to-night. You must see my creation."

He dropped his bantering, mocking tone. He knew well how to arouse the young Baron's interest; that feverish thirst for occult knowledge, that in the old University days had attracted the master's notice, and given him such a willing and ambitious assistant. One, indeed, who had come near to outstripping the very man who taught him. His heart beat with excitement as he saw the interest light up in Henry's eyes: as Henry asked, with an eagerness that in spite of himself he could not conceal:

"Have you also succeeded in bringing life to the dead?

The Professor smiled, quick to detect the note of interest that had crept into the young man's voice: not had he failed to observe that the enmity had quite faded. In Henry's eyes was only that blazing thirst for knowledge that had first attracted the attention of Dr. Pretorius, when they were master and pupil together in the old University days.

The older man smiled, as he murmured with gentle mockery:

"If you, Herr Baron, will do me the honour of visiting my humble abode, I think you will be interested in what I have to show you. You see, after twenty years of scientific research, and so many failures that I daren't think of them, I also have created Life, as we say . . . in God's own image!"

His voice was trembling with pride; and Henry, staring at his pale face and blazing eyes, asked eagerly:

"I must know . . . when can I see it?"

The Professor nodded, smiling once more.

"Ah! I thought you might change your mind. Well, why not to-night? After all," he took an old heavy silver watch from his fob and glanced at it, "it's not very late."

Henry, half-persuaded, asked, "Is it far?"

"Not far," said Dr. Pretorius. "Come, let us go. But you will need a coat."

As Henry clambered out of bed, and walked over to a wardrobe, the Doctor continued, "I'm so glad you've decided to be sensible about it. After all, it isn't often that two brains such as ours have a chance of collaborating. Singly, we have gone further than any men before us: together, and there's no limit to what we could do."

"No," said Henry, pulling a shirt over his head, "you're right, Doctor. There's *nothing* we couldn't do."

"They tell me," said the other, tapping his snuff box with long, bony fingers, and directing a quizzical glance to where the young man was lacing his shoes, "they tell me that there was a little accident to-night. Ahem! Nothing very serious, I hope?" he asked, in his bantering tones.

"No . . . nothing serious," Henry muttered, knotting his tie at the mirror, and avoiding the Professor's eye.

"Good. I'm glad to hear it. Just a little town gossip I suppose."

Henry grinned. "Hardly that, Doctor. Actually, something *did* go wrong. The man I made . . . well," he shuddered . . . "oh don't let's talk about it." He slipped on his jacket, and took a heavy cloak from the cupboard. "Well, Professor, are you ready?"

"When you are," said the other, courteously:

"Good . . . then let us go."

CHAPTER VII

A VOICE FROM THE PAST . . . SO LIFE CLIMBS . . .

AS Henry Frankenstein sat by Dr. Pretorius in the swiftly moving carriage, he wondered into what fantastic adventure his old professor was leading him.

31

He glanced aside at the immobile face, and wondered that such calm should mask those supercilious features: that short, contemptuous upper lip; that long, supercilious nose: those piercing, yet heavy-lidded and insolent eyes.

Henry remembered their first meeting: and encounter in the chemical laboratory of the university, where Henry for months had been working on the preservation of living tissues, after the animal from which they had been taken was dead. Wrapped in thought, he had been standing before the heated glass case, in which, with a steady, uncanny regularity, the heart of a chicken removed five weeks ago from the bird, still beat out the rhythm of life. And as he had watched, dropping from a glass beaker, drop by drop, a nutrifying solution into the liquid in which the heart was immersed, so a voice behind him has asked:

"And to what, Herr Baron, is all this experimentation leading?"

Henry had started, wrapped as he was in the immediate need of keeping life in these unnatural entities, which his science had preserved and endowed with artificial existence. Yet he was not unmindful of the compliment that was paid him by the Professor, in evincing such interest in his own particular hobbies.

So, courteously, he had answered: "To what is it leading, Herr Professor?"

The older man had smiled to hear him answer one question with another. He had shaken his head and wagged a long bony finger at his pupil as he said:

"You heard me, Herr Baron. I asked you to tell me to what end all this experimenting was leading. Surely you have something in view?"

He paused, awaiting an explanation. But Frankenstein had shaken head, and with a smile for an apology.

"I'm sure I don't know. Does one always have an end?"

"A scientist—yes!"

"But, must a scientist always have an end to attain?"

The Professor had nodded.

"Yes . . . if he be a scientist. Otherwise he is simply an experimenter, or . . . oh, no! worse than that! He is simply the man who puts his hand into the bran-pie at Midsummer Fair."

"So. . . !"

"Of course! But I know you well enough to know that this is no idle speculation or curiosity which leads you to preserve the heart of a chicken which used to lay such good eggs all the summer." He laid his finger along the side of his nose, and winked at Henry in mock disapproval. "It must have been for a very good reason that you interfered with the quality of our omelettes!"

Henry had laughed, and shrugged his shoulder.

"Well . . . is it so?"

"Is what what?"

"Is it," the Professor had asked patiently, "the fact, that what you are doing now has the profoundest bearing on what you hope one day to do?"

Henry had hesitated long before answering: but the Professor's glance had been so steady; his question so unequivocal; that the younger man, with a shrug had, at last answered:

"Well . . . I see that it is impossible to conceal from *you,* Herr Professor.

Dr. Pretorius had smiled.

"So! I have (you will pardon, I am sure, the presumption) heard that before. But," he added, with mock humility, " it is only in the hope that my poor knowledge may avail you something, that I dare intrude upon your experiments."

Henry had smiled, not deceived by the Professor's sugary tones.

"Dr. Pretorius, I think I had better be frank with you. Shall I?"

"Perhaps it would be better. . ."

"Very well. May I explain what I have done so far?"

"I am all ears."

"Exactly," Henry said with a manner that was a subtle mockery of the Doctor's own, "You observe here this heart—this chicken's heart. Watch it closely."

The Professor had observed the contents of the bottle for several seconds. Then he had said quietly, unemotionally, "It is beating."

"Yes," Henry had said, not without a certain gratification in his voice, "it is beating. It is alive. . . ."

"*Really* alive?"

"Yes, *really* alive. You will observe that the main arteries are connected up to these silver tubes. Those tubes are connected, in turn, with this small reservoir, from which, by means of this clockwork, blood is circulated through this artificial vascular system!"

"Ah!"

Henry had continued:

"The blood is renewed daily; for I have not yet discovered how to cause it to remain fresh: but the liquid in which the heart itself is suspended, is a chemical compound, which imitates as closely as possible the elementary properties of a chicken's normal diet."

"Yes. . . ?"

"Well, Professor. What I am looking for is this . . . but first of all, let me show you something else." He had led the Doctor to another case in which a shapeless piece of what looked like raw flesh was immersed. "Pancreatic tissue. Nine weeks it has been here. *And it is still alive.* More than that: it is growing. . . ."

He had turned to face the Professor: his eyes glowing with an almost fanatical light.

"Don't you see what I'm striving for?"

"Well . . . I think I do. But go on!"

Calmer now, Henry had explained.

"People who seek for immortality concentrate their attention on life, rather than on death. People say 'If only we understood Life', when they really intend to say 'Could we but analyse the processes of Death!'"

The Doctor had smiled at the young man's earnest tone: but it was a smile that held nothing of mockery; only a tender sentimental remembrance for a student of twenty-five years before, who, in this very laboratory, had occupied his mind with such speculations; and resolved with a fine enthusiasm, to devote his life to their pursuit. He had murmured:

"Baron, you interest me profoundly. Please go on."

Henry had continued.

"An understanding of Life is not essential to the attaining of immortality—or rather (if you will) the conquest of Death. What Life is, we do not know. It may be we never shall know. But what Death is, that we may well discover. . . ."

"Have you discovered what it is?"

With a wry smile, Henry had shaken his head.

"Not altogether. Yet I begin to perceive where my searching may lead. I see the path before me, and my feet well planted there: though what the end is, I cannot, as yet, see clearly."

"But," he had added, "I think I can see an underlying principle in all this haphazard business we call 'living'. But look first of all: here in these bottles are portions of what was once a living thing: a complete organ, and a part of tissue: both essential parts of the complex organism that was once a bird. The one is mechanical. The other exercising its beneficent influences by subtler means, akin to a chemical action, as far as I may judge. Now both these relics are alive: there is not the least doubt that they are living as when they were part and parcel of the hen's body."

"But . . . you have kept them alive."

"So!" Henry had cried, banging the laboratory table with his fist, so that the bottles and retorts jumped and tinkled. "But that is exactly what is so important. I *have* kept them alive: true. That is one way of expressing it. But another way to say it is this: I have given these two part a chance to pursue and independent existence."

Very earnestly he had said: "Professor, I think you will not disagree with me when I say that our ignorance of the nature of Life owes much to a muddled conception of its functions."

"Of course . . . but then, that applies to most things nowadays."

"True . . . but what I intended to say was this: that while people talk glibly of Life on the one hand, and Death on the other, as clearly separate and distinct as chalk from cheese, or night from day: there is, in reality, no such clear division. There are, in other words, two principles of existence: one is the principle of 'living' and the other, the principle of Life. Perhaps I shall make myself more clear if I say that the most complex life forms we know are composed basically of the same materials as the most simple. The one celled amœba, the most primitive form of life we know, is far, far removed from the man created in the proud image of his Divine Maker. But . . . in essence, he yet shares with the lowly amœba the living cell. Only, while the amœba is a unit, man is the aggregation of many millions of cells. In other words man is simply a collection of amœbas . . . is it not so?"

"Yes . . . it is so."

"Very well, then. Now we come to a contradiction in our logic. A man, we have agreed, is a collection of amœbas; a collection of infinitely small living cells: life, in other words, reduced to its lowest common denominator. But . . . and here is the contradiction . . . if I take a thousand million of such animalculae, and heap them together, shall I have made a man?"

He had not waited for an answer, but had continued in his quiet, rapt tones.

"No: I shall not. And yet it was in the contemplation of that certain inability , that the true meaning of life came to me. Life, my dear Professor, is not one, but many-formed. It is, in other words, no more than a name for organization. I say that if I take a hundred thousand amœba and mix them together, I shall not make a man. Yes, but why? Because I am ignorant of the *order* of their assembly. And it is this order which we call Life; that cohesion which binds many units together to form a higher unit. It is this order which we commonly call Life, but which is only one aspect of the spirit of life; which is cohesion, amalgamation—what you will. Life climbs: Life can never be static. And the purpose of Life (which is apparent to us, though we cannot tell shy that purpose should be) is this: that smaller things should band together, and produce of their unity something that lies higher in the processes of creation; and that these higher beings should again amalgamate, and form an entity even higher than the highest among them; and so on, until at last all division ceases, and the wheel comes full circle in the ineffable unity and perfection of GOD."

His voice had been hushed to a whisper, as he said:

"When we die—you and I—it is that order which has made of our myriad component lives, a human being, which dies. For life does not die. Only, the order is broken: the cells scattered; to form order elsewhere; and in their order make some other thing—some body, some plant—we know not what. . . But that is life, the simple indivisible thing, which begins as perfect unity, and strives through coalition with itself, to attain a unity beyond our imagining.

"I talked of cells just now. I used the word 'amœba' figuratively: for if the truth were known—had we a microscope sufficiently powerful; under its peering eye, I doubt not that even the seemingly indivisible amœba would reveal a structure as complex as our own!"

"And . . . ?"

"And this: there is a man in England, Dalton by name, who propounds a startling theory that all matter is composed of infinitely tiny particles, which, small beyond computation, yet by this natural law of cohesion, have made possible all the myriad worlds that sparkle in the evening sky. He affirms that by a process analogous with that by which our universe swings around the sun, and the other universes around those suns we can only guess at, so the particles of the atom swing round a nucleus whose power maintains them in their eternal orbit; an orbit an unvarying as that which produces for us the orderly procession of the Heavens."

"I know. I have read something of this man Dalton's theories. Yet not impossible, I think."

"And I too. Well: to resume. Life then is combination; and each combination marking an advance in harmonic progression towards some ultimate, unthinkable goal. Particles coalesce to form atoms, and atoms coalesce to form cells, while in their varying quantities and orders, these cells combine to form the myriad creatures of the insect, plant, reptile, bird and animal worlds; culminating in the highest expression of known creation: MAN.

"Yet," he had continued, musingly, "Life does not end there. Man is not the summit of creation: not the end of that ladder by which Life climbs. The process of coalition still goes on: man shares with the lowest living thing, that imperative inclination to combine and fuse. Individuals unite into families; families combine into tribes; tribes into nations; and nations into empires and vast confederacies. And . . . observe this, well . . .each higher unit has its own life, its own feelings. A mob is an entity as much as each of the men who compose it: it can think independently of them: just as we can think independently of the germs and cells which compose and regulate our bodies. And not infrequently the mob-thing reasons differently, feels differently, from its components; so that we have the spectacle of a mob formed of quiet, peaceable citizens, burning, violating, murdering; to the great astonishment of those same men.

"There is," the young Baron had said, "a movement to abolish war. I hope it may succeed; but for my part, I doubt it. For wars are not made by men (that is to say, by individuals); they are made by mobs; nations if you like; and the individual has no say in the matter, for it is not by his desire that war happens. Who wants war, who is sensible? Yet wars come, though each man has shrunk from the very idea of war. But at the time when the mob decides, he will go rejoicing; for he is no longer an entity, but a part. What cares the mob for the insignificant *one* of its million parts? Do I spare a thought when I go to the barber for the thousand million cells in his shears will remove from the parent economy? Of course not! Yet, as I said, this is how Life climbs. . . .

"Still," he had murmured, "it seems to me that this is not altogether good. For interdependence becomes a habit after a time, and as Life strives toward that perfected individuality that will come when, not only nations, but worlds and universes be fused together into an entity greater than anything our imagination can conceive, so the individuality of the unit dies, as it joins other units to form a greater.

"Society is as yet only in its infancy, but already we can see the State becoming paramount: already we may see order becoming a habit instead of an ideal, as the 'Mortal God' of the Commonwealth grows to maturity. Ages hence, a man will be incapable of anything but collective thought and collective action. The individual will be an incapable of independent existence as, in the ordinary way, his heart could exist independently of the body for which it supplies the very blood which kept it alive. You say that it is impossible that man should ever be reduced to so subordinate a position. . . ."

"I did not say any such thing. . . ."

"No: not *you*. But most people would say that. Yet what man in all the history of the world has ever meant so much to society as man's own heart means to him? Yet it has no separate existence: it is only by creating an artificial dependence for it, in the shape of this mental vascular system, that it will consent to go on living. . . . Yet, something seems to point to success. Have you seen the kidney?"

"No. . . ."

"Then come." Henry had led the Professor to a small glass case, in which a human kidney was immersed. From this organ had sprouted a multitude of wires and tubes, as with the heart. "Well, Professor . . . look carefully!"

"I see nothing."

"Of course not." A smiling shrug. "There is nothing to see. Yet that kidney is living without artificial stimulus of any sort—except of course its food. I have even taught it how to fear—all by itself. I put a rod into the glass, and poke it, and it sends adrenalin out to sustain the courage of the body which has ceased to exist. . . Fascinating, don't you think?"

"And where is all this leading?" Henry has not missed the fever-bright eyes, and the trembling voice. For a long moment he had gazed into the fevered eyes of his master, while the compact was made between them: not less full and binding because no word was spoken. At last Henry had said, with quiet emphasis:

"I would like to separate life into its constituent parts . . . and then build it up again. Only . . . I should like each part to retain its individuality even in a corporate existence." Very slowly now: "I wonder what that man would be whose heart beat, not only for him, but for itself: Whose eyes, tongue, brain pursued their *own* existence as well as providing him with the means to pursue *his!* Eh, Professor?

And then, in that quiet laboratory, the compact had been sealed between them. For twenty-five years the Doctor had been pursuing the same wild dream; and now, here in the very laboratory where he himself had first conceived the same fantastic possibility, his young pupil had stumbled on that same tempting thought on which he had spent his own youth and fortune.

CHAPTER VIII

THE DREAM MAGNIFICENT. A PACT IS MADE

WELL, the experiment had been made: that weird creature had been constructed out of a hundred different parts; and each living part coördinated into a common life by means of the galvanic battery. They had seen what had happened. Henry's idle speculation had been answered, and in a manner more tragic and terrifying than either could possibly have foreseen.

That idle question: "I wonder what that man would be?" had been answered only too well; and murder and rapine were the earnests of that answer.

But the human mind is a hardy thing. Bitterness and failure, disappointments and loss; these are the things which nourish and preserve, rather than destroy it.

"The dream, my dear Baron," said Dr. Pretorius, "is magnificent enough to be worth a little difficulty in attainment."

That was what Henry thought, too; for he answered, quietly, though not without a certain irony in his voice:

"You know me too well, Doctor. . . ."

There was a chuckle.

"Well, I should say so. But then, didn't we work together; sharing our discoveries; checking each successive step, before we went on to the next?"

In the chill morning air, the hoofbeats of the trotting horses rang out sharp and clear. Henry pulled his cloak closer to him, and the long nose of the Professor was buried in a woollen muffler which he wore.

"Is it far?" Henry asked.

"Not now. My humble abode is not far from here." He chuckled as he saw the distaste on the young man's face; for by this time they were entering the meaner part of the town, where gabled houses overhung streets of rough cobbles, whose open gutters were choked with refuse of every shape and form.

"You don't like my quarters, then?"

"I haven't seen them yet," Henry answered tactfully.

"No . . . but, I mean—the environs. . . ." He waved his bony hand in a comprehensive gesture, and Henry laughed.

"Well! There's many a good wine in a dusty bottle. . . ."

"Yes, that's true!" The Doctor nodded: "I'm comfortable enough where I am. Bachelor establishment, you know . . Hee, hee! And positively no one to interfere."

"Yes," he continued, in a musing voice, "a single life has its advantages. Now, I dare say," the mocking tones went on "that the Baroness Elizabeth has conceived quite a dislike of me." He nodded his head, as if in the relish of some exquisite and unsharable jest. "Yes, fancy that! A nice, quiet, respectable old bachelor like me. . . Ah, here we are!"

Henry, roused from his reverie (for, to tell the truth, he had not been listening to the Doctor's musings), looked out of the window. The carriage had drawn up in front of a house which, though no better preserved than its shabby neighbours, yet evinced, in the richness of the carved brackets that supported the portico, and the fine linen-fold panels on the front door, a certain quality of comfort, of opulence almost, that was lacking in the other houses of that sorry street.

As though aware that Henry was examining the outside of his dwelling with a certain interest, the Doctor said:

"A pity I have no money to spend on the place: for really, when all's said and done, it's rather a fine old place, don't you think?"

"Decidedly out of company with the rest," said Henry, with a shudder.

"Of course," said the Doctor idly, slipping out of the coach with a mincing air, as he gave a delicate finger to the footman who was holding the step.

As Henry alighted, the Doctor said, "I think your coachman had better wait here."

Henry gave the order, and together they stood beneath the bracketed hood which overhung the short flight of steps leading up to the front door.

Producing an enormous key, which he thrust with a lot of noise into an ancient hand-forged lock, the Doctor said:

"I little thought when I first interested myself in your work—ten years ago, wasn't it?—that you would go so far.

"It was nothing," Henry murmured, not unaffected by the Doctor's flattery.

"While I," said the quiet confident voice, "have not been altogether idle! Nor, indeed completely unsuccessful. . . ."

"You must show me everything."

The old Professor laughed.

"Oh, but I will . . . *everything* . . . hee, hee!"

He stood aside as the door opened, and motioned Henry to precede him.

"Go in, Herr Baron. Stand just inside."

Henry stepped gingerly into the pitch black gloom of the hall, his hands outstretched lest he should bang into the furniture with which he felt this place to be most untidily littered.

The voice behind him said: "Walk on for a few yards: the hall is quite empty."

Henry continued his uncertain advance. He heard the door close, and then the noise re-echoed through the old house. Then, as with arms out-stretched, he made a gingerly progress, of a sudden his eyes were blinded with a light as strong and clear as the light of day.

No lamps or candles could have been lit with that astonishing celerity; and in an amazement not altogether untinged with alarm, he turned to find the Professor grinning at him; his hand on a metal lever set in the wall. From above came a hissing and spluttering, that was somehow, in that desolate place, strangely disquieting.

Shielding his eyes from the fierce bluish-white glare, Henry glanced up at the ceiling, where what seemed to be a ball of white-hot metal danced between two black rods, placed point to point. For a second he gazed astonished at this miracle: then turned away lest his sight leave him. He turned blinded eyes to the Doctor.

"What . . . is it?"

"Oh, very simple," said the Doctor, blandly. "The room on your right is filled with electric cells, of the pattern that Italian fellow Volta advocated. Very good pattern, too. Incredibly powerful: though I regret that there's no unit of electrical force as yet. I must see about establishing one. . . ."

Henry interrupted with the cur, "But the light, man? How does it work?"

"Oh yes," the Professor murmured, as though the miraculous light were the most natural thing in the world, "of course! Now let me see:

yes, you did attend my physics lectures, didn't you? Well, this is what I have discovered. If an electrical circuit is broken, and the points of the two wires at the break be advanced sufficiently near, the air will act as a conductor, and a spark will leap across. But you knew that, naturally ..?"

"Yes, I knew that. . . ."

"Well," said the Professor, with an air that would have been ludicrously pedagogic, had Henry not been so intensely interested. "I discovered that with carbon (carbon is an excellent conductor, you know) the same thing happened. Only . . . the spark ignited the positive pole of the 'arc' (as I call it) and raised the particles to a state of incandescence—which is the light you see. So simple, isn't it?"

"So simple," Henry echoed ". . . and so marvellous!"

"The only drawback is this," the Professor continued, "after a time the carbon becomes so eaten away, that the distance between the electrodes becomes too great for the spark to bridge. But I overcame that difficulty by mounting one carbon in a clockwork movement, which advances it, as quickly as it burns away, to meet its partner."

"The light dazzled me at first," said Henry.

"All light does," the Professor answered, sententiously.

"This light more so than others," Henry smiled. "Is all the house lit so miraculously? Is night unknown here?"

"No, Herr Baron. I use this arc-light to give me a little safety. God knows there is nothing by which a robber or thief might profit—but lawless men live in this neighbourhood; and where there is but the light of tallow candle or Argand lamps, there are corners which are dark pools of shadows: and in those shadows a man may lurk. . . ."

"Ah! of course! But," said Henry, "this surely would bring you a fortune were you to put the secret out to manufacture. It is infinitely superior to this new-fangled coal gas: it is brighter, quicker, and (as far as I may judge) quite odourless. . . ."

"I think not," was the indifferent answer. "You see, Baron, while it certainly promises those advantages, there are other reasons which make it hardly a commercially marketable notion. One must be able to rely on an illuminating agent, not an hour, or a day, but for many years. The margin of reliability is not great enough. If the clockwork fails: if I forget to wind the motor, the light will fail. And besides, the noise is excessive."

"At first; but even after this short time, I hardly perceive it. It is no worse than living by a mil-race. . . ." He broke off, shuddering. That word 'mill' was as yet possessed of too dreadful a significance that he should utter it lightly.

"Will you go upstairs?" said the Doctor. "My study is there."

Slowly Henry mounted the staircase, which was broad, with wide, shallow stairs. Half way up, there was a small landing, where the stairs turned, hiding the wall from view.

Henry heard the Doctor's voice behind him.

"There's a light in my study: I'll wait and put this one out . . ." and then, from the *top of the stairs*, he heard the same voice:

"Herr Baron, you walk slowly, to-night. Will you come up, please?"

There was mockery in the tones; and Henry, seized with a sudden panic, rushed back to the landing, peering over the balustrade into the hall below. But there was the Doctor, as he had left him, standing by the lever which controlled the light.

As he saw Henry, his eyebrows went up.

"Hallo!" he said, "What are *you* looking for?"

Henry, recovered a little from his alarm, snapped: "I want to know how you could have got upstairs so quickly. Are you a ventriloquist as well as a scientist?"

"Both," was the quiet answer. "Look!"

He turned to a small wooden box fixed on the wall just inside the front door. It was hard for Henry to see anything of its construction, but there appeared to be a round hole in the front side. Against this hole, the Doctor applied his lips. Then from upstairs, came a voice, like the Doctor's, but huskier, deeper altogether.

"Come upstairs, Herr Baron: this instrument is even simpler than the others."

Henry laughed, and did as he was invited. Behind him, the sputtering arc-light was extinguished, and he heard Pretorius's feet stumbling on the oaken stairs.

"Can't you," he called out, "Make yourself a pocket lamp, Doctor?"

"I have," the old man grumbled, "but it burnt my fingers. So I use my old tinder box and matches instead. It's safer. My study's the first door on the left."

Henry opened the door and went in.

As the Doctor came into the room, he said:

"Sit down, Herr Baron, sit down. Make yourself comfortable."

Henry sat down; staring around him, while the Doctor busied himself in an adjoining room.

It was an extraordinary place in which the young man found himself: though well in keeping, as he admitted, with the known character of the Professor.

It had once, this study, been a room of magnificent proportions. The ceiling was still lofty, and the embrasures of the lattice windows deep: but at some time or other, a screen of rough planks had been erected to divide the room into two parts, and spoiling altogether its symmetrical proportions.

But what was left made a study admirably spacious: although none to spacious for the multitudinous trappings of the Doctor. A huge oaken table sagged beneath the weight of countless leatherbound volumes, and a quantity of scientific instruments and appliances: alembics, retorts, beakers full of liquids of many colours, and, at one end, a nest of Voltaic cells.

There were a number of chairs; but these, too, were used solely for bearing a weight of books and papers; and practically every square inch of the floor, besides the shelves, were littered with books.

The Doctor's hat was placed on a skeleton's shiny pate; and on a small table was the half-dissected body of a cat.

"A cheerful sort of home," Henry murmured as the Doctor returned with a bottle and two glasses. He cleared the portion of the table nearest to Henry by the simple expedient of sweeping everything, with a single movement of his arm, on to the floor. He placed the glasses on the table, and drew the cork from the bottle with his teeth.

"Herr Baron," he said, pouring out the spirit, "before I show you the results of my trifling experiments, I would like to drink to our partnership. Do you like gin? It is," he simpered, "my only weakness."

"Thank you," Henry said, drawing his glass towards him, "provided," he smiled, "that it is the gin I am used to."

"I think," the Doctor said, "that you need not fear for the quality of the gin, even though it is true that we do not all live at the Schloss Frankenstein!"

"Oh, come, my dear Doctor," Henry chided, "I did not mean to offend you. I only wondered," he said with twinkling eyes, "whether this gin might not have been made out of door-knobs or beaver-hats, by some new electrical process.

The Doctor, mollified, shook his head, smiling.

"Taste it . . . and see."

Henry sipped at the potent spirit: and laughed.

"I see it is not . . . yet there is nothing I would not credit after to-night."

He asked, sitting in his chair: "Tell me, Professor, of that strange voice I heard to-night . . . how was it contrived?"

"Oh, *that* . . . ? Quite simple, my dear Baron. I use it to give my orders to the tradesmen's boys: (I always leave my front door open in the summer). They of course think I am speaking through a hole in the wall." He got up from his chair, and went over to a cupboard. "I'll show you *my* end of the instrument."

Henry watched him unfasten a small box about the size of a household medicine chest, from two wires, and lay it carefully on the table.

"I'll unscrew the front panel; and you will then be able to see how it works. Ah! . . . now let me show you!"

Henry leant forward; while the Professor, with a pencil, indicating the various parts.

"This, Herr Baron, is an instrument of speech: but my model was the human ear. Strange, was it not, that the organ of hearing was my model for an instrument of speech?"

"They are the same thing," said Henry.

"Oh, so you know that? True, true," he muttered. "Well, this is the secret. This upright square frame of wood is covered with a membrane of gold-beater's skin. Directly in the centre of the membrane you observe a little piece of metal. That is silver foil pasted on to the membrane. From that piece of foil a wire is led off—but of that later. Now, at the back of the membrane is this upright metal rod, through which a thumbscrew turns. If I turn it—so!—the point will meet the piece of silver foil. See, I adjust it delicately. There must be no pressure on the screw on the membrane. The metal point and the silver foil must just meet.

"That screw is also connected by a wire, to a battery of cells; and from the metal foil, the wire goes to the other pole of the battery; passing on its way through an instrument exactly similar to this. Now, what happens when I speak against the diaphragm? It vibrates, exactly as the air is set in motion by my larynx. The membrane vibrates; the contact between point and foil is broken, and foil on the other instrument is also broken.

"What happens? I say 'Here . . . !' " From below a faint "Here!" came to their ears. "You see? I break the contact with my voice, and the instrument below reverses the procedure: it reproduces my voice as the contact is broken!"

He took the box and replaced it carefully in the cupboard. "My electric cells gave me the most trouble. I started off with Volta's *'Couronne de tasses,'* and later went on to use his copper and zinc pile. But that was not altogether satisfactory. It was not constant enough for delicate work. At the present time, I am using a cell consisting of pure mercury covered with a paste made by boiling mercurous sulphate with a saturated solution of zinc sulphate. On this paste, I next rest a zinc plate. The mercury, of course, acts as a negative plate. I find it quite satisfactory. It is certainly very constant."

Henry said gently: "Why did they ask you to leave the University? The fools! 'Blind mouths'—as an English poet once called their tribe!"

The Doctor's mouth was a thin line as he shrugged his shoulders, and murmured: "You ask a question as old as the world. Why did they imprison Galileo, and why did the father of Human Wisdom drink deep of hemlock? Because, my dear pupil of a happier time, such men as these of whose company am I, are born out of their time. We come with full hands, and the world is not ready for our gifts. Galileo was more fortunate than the Marquess of Worcester, for, although the great Italian suffered imprisonment, and endured the humiliation of a forced 'recantation,' yet at least he received the due acknowledgement of his discovery. Worcester was not so fortunate. In his prison, his active genius devised a steam engine; but the time was not yet ripe, and many years had to pass before someone else 'discovered' the principle once more.

"There is a young man at present superintending engineering operations for the French Emperor; who has applied the steam engine with considerable success to the propelling of vessels. I met him in Paris in '96 or '98, I forgot now which. On no, it must have been '98, because all that troublesome Revolution had died down. Yes, that was the year . . . Well, as I say, he has taken the inventions of two men (although who invented the ship I really cannot say) and lo and behold! He becomes the inventor of the steam-ship!"

Henry could not help laughing at the Professor's half-humorous indignation.

He said: "But so he is!"

"Bah! What has he invented! No . . . it is the way of the world, where rogues pick the brains of honest men. One of these days someone will invent an electric lamp, and a voice-carrier. And that will be when the world is ready for it."

He yawned, and thrust out his thin legs in their rather shabby trousers.

"Well," he said, stretching out his arms, "to work! Let me show you my experiments—or rather, my successes."

He raised his glass.

"To a new world of Gods and Monsters," he said, tossing off the dregs of the spirit with every evidence of enjoyment. "The creation of Life," he mused, rising from his chair, "is distinctly enthralling, is it not? I cannot," he said lightly, "account precisely for all that I am going to show you, but perhaps now that you are my partner—*you* can."

There was something in the quiet tones, some sinister implication in that last "*you* can . . ." that suddenly sent a chill down Henry's spine, so that the room seemed on an instant, hot and stifling. He slipped off his overcoat, and with nervous fingers unloosed the muffler around his neck. He had the same feeling as many years before had possessed him: a small boy who was being taken by his father to see the Medical Museum at Nüremberg. That same imminence of horror . . . and worse, inescapable horror. . . .

But . . . well . . . what was to be, would be. *Cher sara, sara:* as the Italians said. Henry had the feeling that he was too deeply embroiled in all this business to think of freedom. It was too late now. He knew it, he must go on: to whatever end awaited him.

"At least," he whispered, "it will have been an adventure worth the daring."

There was a shuffling step outside the door, and the Doctor entered.

"I didn't see you go out," said Henry.

"I went to get my . . . my experiments. . . ."

He placed the box he was carrying carefully down on the table. It was covered with a black cloth; but with his fingers grasping a corner, the Doctor said:

"My experiments did not turn out quite like yours—Henry—but Science, like Love, has her little surprises—as you shall see."

He pulled the cloth gently off; and from the box he took six glass jars, placing them with delicate finical care, side by side on the table.

"Good Heavens, Doctor!" Henry gasped, "what, in the name of our Creator, are *these?*"

He stared in a sort of fascinated horror at the jar nearest to him, in which a human being—or what seemed to be a human being—was sitting. She was dressed in the robes of a Queen: in velvet and ermine, and she sat on a carven throne. Yet whoever had seen a woman like this: who, though perfectly proportioned, stood but seven inches high! But that this was no mere marionette was clearly apparent. For as his bewildered glance ran over her small, shapely body, the little Queen made a graceful curtsey.

The Doctor laughed, his bony finger with its long, dirty nail, tapping the lid.

"There is a pleasing variety in my exhibits. My first experiment, this one. She was so lovely that I made her a queen."

He picked up the jar, and held it up to his eyes.

"Don't you think I was right? Isn't she charming?" He said, lifting the cover of the second jar: "Then of course, we had to have a King."

Henry laughed. The mannikin had been dressed in outrageous imitation of that King Henry of England, whose wives and whose gluttony had made him famous even in that remote German barony. And as though the homunculus had taken on with his kingly habiliments some of the character of his illustrious (or notorious, if you prefer) prototype, he was devouring a chicken's leg (as big to him as an ox's, almost) with a gluttonous abandon that caused Henry to remark:

"His character seems much in keeping with his dress."

"You haven't, fortunately, seen how much!"

He picked up another jar. "Now this, my dear Baron, is the very devil … Very bizarre, this little chap! There's a certain resemblance to me, don't you think? Or do I flatter myself?" He sighed, as he put the jar down, and the miniature devil shook his tiny pitchfork at his maker. "I took a great deal of pains with him. Sometimes, I have wondered whether life wouldn't be much more amusing if we were all devils—with no nonsense about being devils … and about being good. …"

His soliloquizing was cut short by Henry's sudden shout.

"Look!" he cried, pointing to a little figure which was racing across the table towards the jar in which the Queen was seated.

"Dear, dear!" the Doctor said impatiently, "that King is really too outrageous! I left the top off, and he must have climbed out!"

He took a pair of tweezers out of his breast pocket, and picked the King up. The little figure waved its arms and legs as it was borne through the air. Then, none to gently, he was dropped back into the jar.

"Even royal amours can be a nuisance," the Doctor said as he replaced the lid.

The Queen had been watching all this by-play, and an Archbishop in another jar was turning a disapproving eye on the royal pair.

"Poor Archbishop," said the Doctor, "he has his hands full here; I can assure you." He took a cloth, and threw it over the King's jar. "There, that will keep him quiet. My ballerina now, is charming: but, oh! such a bore. She won't dance for anything but a certain minuet of Scarlatti's;

and it get so *very* monotonous. My next, I am afraid, is rather conventional—but one can never tell how these thing will turn out . . . it is an experiment with seaweed. Normal size, as you will observe, has been my great difficulty."

He picked up the jar, and Henry, examining its contents in the dim candle light could not withhold a gasp of admiration. For sitting on a tiny rock, her little naked feet sunk in golden sand, was a mermaid. Her upper body, with its delicate maidenly curves, was pure woman, while from her waist the iridescent scales of a fish glittered opal in the yellow flame of the candle. In one hand she held a mirror, and with the other she was passing a comb through her long golden tresses.

"Well?" the Doctor asked.

Henry shook his head. "I don't know *what* to say. It's amazing!"

He thought of the ungainly, lumbering body that he had created: that nightmare thing men called "The Monster." In his mind's eye, he saw that dull, inhuman face, with its scarred and riveted scalp; and he compared it with these warm, graceful figures in the jars before him.

He heard Pretorius say: "You did achieve size. I need to work that out with you. . . ."

He shook his head.

"But, Professor, this isn't science. It's more like black magic!"

The old Doctor pursed his thin lips, as he bent his piercing gaze on his young companion.

"You think I'm mad," he muttered. "Well," ignoring Henry's gesture of dissent; "perhaps I am . . . But listen, Henry Frankenstein. While you were digging in your graves, snatching limb and bone and sinew from the cadavers there; piecing the dead tissues together, and welding the dead flesh into a monstrous lampoon of the living; I, my dear pupil, went for *my* materials to the very source of life. . . ."

Henry stared, only half comprehending what the other was saying. "You mean. . . ."

"I mean that I grew my creatures like cultures: grew them as Nature does—from seed."

Henry had sunk down into a chair, his elbows resting on the table, his chin cupped in his hands. He said: "After this, you must tell me why they made you leave the University. I heard things, you know . . . But, one doesn't always give credence to tales" and the tales were very wild."

"Yes, I shall be pleased to tell you. It was nothing infamous. Only. . . well—only a little *unusual*, say."

Henry said: "Tell me more of these cultures of yours."

"Oh, yes, the cultures . . . Yes, as I said, I grew them as Nature does—from seed. I studied the growth of the human body: not from birth, but from the very moment when the female seed is fertilized in the mother's body. Many years I spent in research; for anatomical dissection is unfortunately not yet included in the curriculum of our medical schools, and my practical work was not too easy to come by.

"Still, I managed somehow to learn what I wanted. And then, when not only each stage in existence was clear in my mind, but more, the *reasons* why each stage should and must succeed the preceding one,—the artificial germination of the human protoplasm then, and then only, did I begin my great experiment.

"I constructed an electrically-heated incubator, in which I reproduced, as nearly as possible, the conditions of nature. Yet I did all this by artificial means: there were no human organs preserving an independent existence! Hee, hee! None of that, my dear Baron.

"And as clean as you like. Most important that. I'm only just beginning to realize the danger of physical uncleanliness. And the things we tolerate! Our sewers, flies, horses in the streets: dogs, and their disgusting habits! Good Lord, once you begin to appreciate these things, you begin to wonder how life survives at all. The progress of medicine lies in the abolition of dirt. When dirt goes, most of our troubles will go with it. . . ."

Henry said, with a smile (thinking of the Doctor's finger-nails): "And the incubation?"

"Oh . . . I was forgetting! Yes, that went all very well—at first. But then, some mistake, for which I can't account, upset the timing arrangements. I realized that the embryo was growing too fast: that that change we call 'quickening' which in ordinary pregnancies happens about mid-term, was occurring at the end of the third *week!* In six weeks the embryo was fully grown. Curious, isn't it?"

"Very curious," said Henry, looking at the Queen, who was smiling at him in a most brazen way.

"What do you make of it?"

"Of what?"

"Of the shortness of the term. Can you account for it?"

Henry shook his head.

"Off-hand . . . no, I can't. But a solution may suggest itself, with careful experiment. How old are they now?"

"Two years, and they're fully adult. I give them about five years. The same as a rat. Period of gestation is about the same, too."

"It's wonderful!" said Henry, for the tenth time that evening.

"I suppose so," said the Doctor idly, gathering up the jars, and replacing them in their box. "But, still: you did achieve results that I have missed. Now, think what a world-astonishing collaboration we can be." He added, "You and I together! Yes, Henry?"

The young man shook his head.

"No?"

"Oh no, no, no!"

"And why not, indeed?"

"You don't understand. . . Think what I've been through. . . ."

The Doctor shrugged, a faint sneer on his lips.

"For science, my dear Baron: for science? You don't begrudge a few little sacrifices made for *her,* surely?"

Henry said:

"You call them *little sacrifices* : that children were murdered, and I almost with them?

Pretorius laughed. "As the English say 'a miss is as good as a mile.' You weren't murdered; and that's the end of it. . . ."

"Is it? I wonder. . . ." He added, thoughtfully, "it seems to me as though it might almost be the beginning."

"Henry" said the Doctor, with unwonted seriousness, "you said 'No' just now, when I suggested a partnership. Why? Did you think that there are mistakes which can never be rectified? I assure you that there are none. Come," he said, "leave the charnel-house and follow the lead of Nature—or of God, if you like your Bible stories: 'male and female created him them,' 'be fruitful and multiply.' Let us obey the Biblical injunction: you, of course, have the choice of natural means; but as for me, I am afraid that there is no course open to me but the scientific ways." He chuckled throatily: "Let us create a new race—a man-made race, upon the face of the earth. Why not?"

"Oh, Doctor, I daren't! I daren't even think of such a thing!"

The older man continued, as though he had not heard Henry's wild protest.

"Our mad dream is only half realized. Alone, you have created a man. . . ." He leaned forward, and Henry shrank from the fanatical glare in those staring eyes. "Now, together," he whispered, "we shall create his mate!"

"You mean. . . ."

"Yes," simpered the Doctor, quite in his ordinary manner, "a woman.

That," he giggled, "should be *really* interesting.

There was no answer, only Henry shook his head in a sort of dazed wonder.

"Bah!" said the Doctor, "we shall be famous yet: you mark my words."

He struck heavily on an old-fashioned brass gong that stood by his chair.

"You'd like some coffee before you return. The dawn's inclined to be chilly."

"Oh," said Henry, "please don't bother. . . ."

"No bother, my dear Baron, no bother, Ah, Franz: there you are!"

Henry turned to the door in amazement: and what he saw did nothing to quieten the fears with which, ever since he had entered this gloomy, sinister dwelling, he had been filled. For, standing just within the doorway, was the most hideous hunchback that Henry had ever seen. Not only was his body twisted and contorted into a hideous mockery of the human form; but on his face, with its low brow, and projecting frontal ridge; its sloppy, swollen lips, through which the grimy, yellow buck-teeth protruded, the countenance of this creature presented every mark of depravity and crime. Henry shrank back from the monstrous implications of that perverted visage.

But the Doctor seemed not in the least aware of anything unusual in the appearance of his servant; for with a graceful wave of the hand, he said:

"Franz, this the Freiherr von Frankenstein. You will please obey him as you do me."

The creature leered, and made a horrible sort of shuffling movement, as with one twisted arm it pulled its forelock in a grotesque gesture of respect.

"Coffee, please, Franz; *and quickly.*"

In spite of his disquietude, Henry could not refrain from smiling at the Doctor's imperious tones, and at the celerity with which the order was obeyed. The Doctor said, quietly: "I can see that my servant does not please you. A little *farouche* of appearance, perhaps? Ah, well, they cannot always be beautiful, and Zeus must have had other cupbearers than Ganymede. And not less efficient, I dare say!"

"Where did you get him?" Henry asked.

"He's an original," the Professor answered irrelevantly.

"I can see that. But, tell me, how did you find him? He seems to be a good servant, in spite of his looks, poor man."

Dr. Pretorius nodded, smiling (but a little grimly, Henry could not help thinking).

"Oh. yes, he's obedient enough. He wouldn't dare be otherwise."

"There's a story behind all this, Doctor."

The Doctor nodded. "Yes . . . quite an interesting one. . . Do you want to hear it?"

"I should like to very much." (Anything to forget the contemplation of his own folly, in agreeing to assist the Doctor's mad schemes.)

"Well," said the Doctor deliberately, "this all happened about the time when I was forced to resign my professorship at the University. Actually it was a very small, small matter. A question of taking a corpse out of the mortuary. You know how difficult it is to get cadavers for dissection. . . ."

"You employed a resurrection man?"

"Of course . . . and there was some trouble about it!"

"I suppose it was someone of good family?" Henry asked.

"No," said the Doctor absently, "it happened that the lady (it was a lady, I forgot to tell you) was in the habit of suffering from cataleptic fits. She had come here from Innsbruck, where the townspeople were quite aware of her malady. But on her first day in Frankenstein, she was seized with a fit in the marketplace and, thinking her dead, they placed her in the mortuary!"

"But how terrible!" Henry cried, "And she was not dead at all."

The Doctor sniggered. "*So they said.* But how was *I* to know?"

"But there were signs; surely?"

The old man nodded absently: "To be sure—when one is looking for them. Curiously enough, I did think the body was rather warm, before I started dissecting."

"And you paid no attention to it?"

"It never occurred to me to realize what had happened."

"No . . . of course not."

"And then," the Doctor continued, still in the same conversational tones, "when she *did* recover, it was too late to do anything about it. You see," he sighed, "I had done quite a lot of dissecting before she screamed. . . ."

"And . . . then. . . ." Henry gasped.

The Doctor shrugged, and spread out his hands.

"Then? Oh, of course, I did the only merciful thing. After all," he simpered, "she wouldn't have liked to go back to her husband with . . . well . . . it was all very awkward."

He leered in a manner impossible to describe, and Henry shuddered.

"The time I had! Why, do you know, my dear Baron, that those ignorant townspeople, the serfs of your father, went so far as to accuse me of murder!" He added indignantly, If it hadn't been for the protection of His Serene Highness the Duke, I daren't think what might have happened. But *Seiner Durchlaucht* is a man of understanding, with a great respect for the *savants.*"

There was a shuffling step outside, and the door was opened by Franz bearing the coffee.

The Doctor rubbed his thin hands, chuckling.

"Ah, good! Made it strong, Franz?"

"Yes!" was the surly answer.

"Yes *Herr Doktor*, the Professor corrected, in high good humour.

"Yes, Herr Doktor."

"That's quite right. Now why didn't you knock on the door as I have ordered you to do, so frequently?"

"I forgot."

"You've no right to forget," said the Doctor, mildly, shaking his head and one raised finger at the same time. "Mustn't forget anything in this house... *anything* ... do you understand?" he added fiercely, with a sudden change of manner.

The hunchback nodded, bitter hatred welling up in his bloodshot eyes.

"If only I could," he mumbled.

"But you never will," the Doctor piped, smiling again. "Now how's the coffee made? Tell the Freiherr, my friend."

The man said in a sing-song voice, in the manner of a child repeating a laboriously conned lesson. "Black as night: sweet as love: hot as hell. . . ."

"Good," the Professor beamed. "Now run away Franz! And don't come listening at key-holes. You might learn something."

When the servant had gone, Henry muttered contemptuously: "Poor devil! Why do you bully him so, Pretorius?"

The Doctor paused in the act of pouring the coffee, and the smile froze on his face. He turned his piercing eyes full on the young man as he said, in quiet tones that held a world of meaning. "Because my life depends on it . . . he would kill me if he feared me less. . . . Sugar Baron?"

"Thank you . . .but why does he hate you so? Could you not have gained his friendship?"

"Never . . . he is without finer feelings."

"Without finer feelings! Then why employ such a man?" Henry said in amazement.

"That is why," the Doctor smiled. "His very indifference to anything but me, makes him an ideal servant . . . especially for me."

Again that chill seemed to run up Henry's spine, as understanding came to him of what the Doctor might ask a servant to do. . . ."

"I was curious," the Doctor said, "how he came to be my servant. Years ago (just after I resigned my Professorship at the University, to be precise) I took lodgings in a street not far from here. Franz was my landlord, and he had a wife, then. Yes,—can you credit it? It's amazing how these ugly creatures find women to marry them! But they do. . . . Well, well. Anyhow, I had been there only a month or two, when I became convinced that the couple had some unpleasant designs toward me. I can't quite explain it: but you know how it is—one feels these things.

"I determined to find out. Now about this time, I was experimenting on my voice-carrier. I had, indeed, perfected it only a week or so before my suspicions became almost certainty. So while the two of them were out, I slipped into the kitchen, and fixed my voice-carrier behind a little shrine, where I knew it would not be detected—at least, for some time."

"And your suspicions were verified?" Henry asked with interest.

"Verified!" The Doctor laughed. "My dear Baron, I locked my door and sat waiting by the instrument in my room. The hours passed, and late that evening I heard footsteps in the street below, and a woman's voice exchanging a 'good-night' with the night-watch; then the sound of the front door being opened, and voices in the hall.

"Franz and his wife had returned!

"You can imagine," the Doctor said, "with what excitement I sat by my instrument, listening to their footsteps retreating down the hall, and finally hearing the sound of the kitchen door shutting.

"Then from my instrument came the tones of the woman's voice, blurred and distorted by the instrument, but still recognizable. I heard her say:

" 'Shall it be to-night, Franz?' and the man said,

" 'I think so, Lisa. I'm tired of waiting for the old rogue's money.'

" 'At what time, then?'

" 'As soon as he's gone to sleep: I'll creep in, and slit his throat.'

There was a pause here, and I could imagine those two beauties grinning at each other. Then:

" 'But suppose he locks his door?'

"I heard Franz laugh: 'He probably has!'

" 'Then we're defeated. . . ! Oh, Franz, why didn't you think of that!"

"Franz said, 'It's fortunate for us that I've got some brains in my head. Yesterday I removed the bolt from the lock. So that, while he can turn the key on me, he can't lock himself in.'

"Baron, imagine how I felt now! To know that I was at the mercy of such scoundrels! Of course, I could shout, but in that neighbourhood, who was there to hear? And the watch had passed on his rounds a quarter of an hour before; which meant that he would not be round again until the dawn. What a predicament! And then I heard Lisa say:

" 'But won't they suspect us of having murdered him?'

" ' No,' Franz chuckled, 'they won't. We shall discover his body in the morning, and find at the same time that we left the front door open by mistake. That mistake, of course, enabled a relative of the poor woman he killed, to enter and revenge himself."

" 'But how will they know it was revenge?"

" 'The murderers will leave a note . . . simple isn't it?' the villain laughed.

" 'Oh, Franz,' I heard the woman say, 'how wonderful you are!'

"The next few hours were the worst in my life. Several times Franz or Lisa would come upstairs, and knock gently on the door; and when I asked what they wanted, answer 'Are you requiring anything. Herr Doktor?' It was as much as I could do to avoid going downstairs, and trying to slip out of the house; but for one thing, I don't think I should ever have reached the front door; and for another, I hate running away.

"At last I decided to arm myself with the poker, and pretend to be asleep. Franz came up again, knocked, and got no answer. In the moonlight, I saw the door open gently, and his head peer in.

"Then, as if satisfied, he nodded and withdrew. I heard him go softly downstairs. As I surmised, he had forgotten his knife. I heard him tell his wife so. Then his footsteps sounded in the hall, as he walked to the bottom of the stair.

" In a few seconds, I realized, I should be fighting for my life. On a sudden impulse, I slipped out of bed, and stood just within the door, grasping my poker, intending, with God's grace, to hit him as he entered the room.

"I shall never forget that wait, as his quiet steps came faintly to my straining ears. He was ascending the staircase with every caution; and I stood there with my heart beating to suffocation, while the moonlight streamed through the latticed panes of the window, and showed me the room, for probably the last time in my life.

"There was the table at which I had sat; the old armchair; my books . . . and . . . Baron, you know how inspiration comes! There was no time to think! I simply slipped quickly to my voice carrier, and whispered into it (expecting every second that the door would open): 'Wicked woman! Is murder the way in which you hope for salvation?"

"I heard a gasp from the instrument, and a babbling voice: 'Oh, Holy Mother of God! Forgive us. . . forgive us . . . we didn't know what we were doing. . . .'

"I said quickly: 'It is not too late. Call you husband; and then both from the instrument and through the house, came a frenzied shouting: 'Franz, Franz!'

"I heard the man say: 'Be quiet, you fool! You'll wake him!' Then her footsteps as she ran up the stairs, and a mixture of oaths and prayers, sobs and curses, as she fought to make him return.

" 'It was the Holy Mother herself; her image spoke to me. . . .'"

" 'Oh nonsense! you hysterical fool.'

" 'Franz, it's true. . . .'"

" 'I don't believe it . . . women's tales! Pah!'

"There was only one thing to do. They could not hear me. I spoke into the voice carrier once more.

" 'Come back, file sinners! Come back while your hands are still clean!'

"I was scared, Baron; but even so, I had to laugh, as I heard their frantic flight down the stairs. But for what happened after that, I don't know. It was my intention to switch off the current; but instead, I must have turned the lever the other way, sending the full force of electric current through the circuit.

"Lisa, downstairs, in a frenzy of fear, must, in the dim light, have touched the metal image, and pushed it against the contact of the voice-carrier. I only know that I heard a sudden scream . . . and Franz's dreadful cry from below, as the woman's body blackened and twisted under that terrible force that can uproot trees or shatter houses.

"In an hour's time I walked quietly downstairs. Franz was sitting on a chair, gazing stupidly at the dead body of his wife. The carving knife which he had intended for my throat, was still lying on the table.

" 'Well,' said I, 'what is all this?'

"He crossed himself: 'Heaven only knows Herr Doktor!'

" 'You are right!' I said sternly. 'Heaven *does* know: and Heaven has interfered with your dastardly plans. *I* know what you intended.' I picked up the knife, and as he shrank back, 'I was thinking of calling the watch; but perhaps . . . if you repent . . . I may forgive you.'

"He signed a full confession, Herr Baron (he was not himself, you understand) and since then, he has divided his time between helping me, and hunting for his confession."

He poured himself some cold coffee. "I hope," he sighed, "that he never finds it."

CHAPTER IX

THE BURGOMASTER'S PRESTIGE HAS NOT SUFFERED

AROUND them, as the blue of night paled into the grey of dawn, the town slept on; happily unconscious of the tragic forces which were not yet laid to rest.

Perhaps they slept the sounder in that they slept the happier for having seen the ancient mill crash in flames, knowing that in its burning it had made a holocaust of any living thing that had remained within.

People had sat up late in Frankenstein that night, describing in a thousand different ways the events of that exciting evening. At the Bear Inn, in the Market Place, the common room was crowded. Among a throng of soldiers, gendarmes, tradesmen and general hangers on, the Burgomaster was describing his plan of campaign and his conduct of that plan with many digressions concerning his own valour.

The Burgomaster was known to be in the confidence of the Castle (though old Baron Frankenstein would have been surprised to hear it) and in those days, with serfdom abolished only a decade before, the respect for authority, even though it were vested in such a windy popinjay as the Burgomaster, still endured.

He was sitting in a high chair, beside the tall oaken grandfather clock which was the pride of the Bear Inn. With a many-ringed hand he was twisting the ends of his long moustache; taking an occasional pull at his heavily-ornamented meerschaum pipe, and a more frequent pull at his pewter-lidded *stein;* and basking in the obvious admiration of his little entourage.

"What a business!" he said, puffing out his cheeks. "What a business indeed! Well, I for one, am glad it's all over."

"You're right there, sir," "I'll bet you are!" and so on.

"What are you going to do about little Maria Kramer?" asked a tall red-faced farmer.

"The little girl who was . . . strangled? Oh, er . . . well, what do you mean exactly?"

"I mean," said the man, "that we ought to do something about her parents. After all, they can't afford to give her a decent funeral."

"Oh *that*?" said the Burgomaster. "I see what you mean. Actually, I was going to suggest a subscription for that very purpose."

"And what about young Baron Henry?" asked another.

"What about him?" the Burgomaster demanded, a little uncertainly.

"They tell me that he's alive."

"Alive! Why man, I saw his dead body myself. What foolish story is this?"

"Well," the man (a grocer) said obstinately, "I'm only saying what's been told to me. I met a footman from the Castle, and he tells me that the young Baron's as right as rain. Only a bit shaken, that's all."

The Burgomaster twisted his moustaches with a nervous hand, and shook his head.

"I don't believe it."

"Well," the man grumbled, "I'm only telling you what. . . ."

"What a garrulous lackey heard in the servants' hall! Fiddlesticks!"

"Well," said another, a woman this time, "it's just as well that the young Baron has gone: God rest his soul! Or he might have had to answer some very awkward questions."

"Oh!" the Burgomaster said sarcastically, "and what questions, pray? And *who* is to ask them?"

"You," the woman answered, flushing, "and what you'll want to know is this: how much truth there is in the story that young Baron Henry had a hand in all this Monster business."

"Woman, don't be a fool!"

"Don't you 'woman' me, Burgomaster! It's common knowledge!"

"And that, of course, entitles it to our greatest respect!" he sneered.

"I don't know about that," was the mumbling replay. "But they do say as how it was a dead man's corpse that killed little Maria Kramer."

"Old wives' tales! How could a dead man walk about?"

"There's such a thing as witchcraft, sir," an old farmer chided gently.

The Burgomaster sighed, and mopped his forehead with a red silk handkerchief.

My dear grandpa," he said, " you're quite wrong there. There's no such thing as witchcraft. Modern science has disproved it."

The old man growled his disbelief of the statement.

"Would you go on the Brocken on Walpurgis Night, Burgomaster?"

"Of course I would. . . ." And then, in a placatory voice, as he realized that the sympathy of the crowd was not altogether his: "I'm not going to say that the Monster wasn't a very unpleasant and frightening sort of madman—but—well, he was a man like any of you. Ghost indeed!"

"Master," said the old man, pulling his forelock and making a profound curtsey, "we didn't say he was no *ghost*. What we said was that he was made up out of dead bodies, and set goin' by magic, like a puppet on the end of a string."

The Burgomaster took a long pull at his tankard. He was rapidly losing patience with this pack of zanies, as in his own mind he called them.

"How could you *possibly* know these things?" he asked indignantly. "*I* haven't heard anything of all this."

"Well it's true," a voice insisted.

"Is it?"

"Yes, it *is!* And . . . if it is, Burgomaster, what are you going to do about it? Are you going to make Baron Henry responsible?"

The Burgomaster nearly choked.

"Shut up, you fool!" he shouted. "Listen, you fools, all of you! If I hear another word about the Monster, I'll clear this inn, and order you all to bed!"

An awkward silence descended on the assembled company, until the Burgomaster had the happy inspiration to discuss Baroness Elizabeth . . . and in five minutes they were once more discussing the Monster.

CHAPTER X

THE NEWS COMES TO FRANKENSTEIN TOWN

AND meanwhile, above the town, in the fields which bordered the dense pine forest, a young shepherdess was tending her sheep. They were drinking at a pond which lay under a small bluff, and on this bluff, overlooking her flock, the little shepherdess sat, swinging her legs.

She was looking across the hillside at the twinkling lights of the town, at the yellow diamonds that were the windows of distant Castle Frankenstein.

So immersed was she in admiring the view (being, indeed, more than a little sleepy) that she did not see the tall gaunt form which came stumbling through the woods, and moving gait of a drunken man.

A hundred yards away from where the girl sat dreaming, the figure stopped at a small waterfall; kneeling down by the side of the mountain rivulet, and scooping up the water in the palm of its hand, drinking ravenously, and grunting like an animal.

It stopped drinking, satiated, and the calm surface of the water showed him a face. It was white, and heavy, and scarred—and as he gazed he struck at it, shattering the image into a thousand fragments.

Then the Monster (for it was he) stumbled to his feet, and set off on his swaying run.

Branches brushed him, and clinging weeds impeded his progress, while brambles tore at face and hands. But always he went foreward, with a blind purposefulness that brooked of no petty diversion.

At last the woods gave way to the open country, and as he crashed out of the pines he stood blinking uncertainly at the prospect before him.

To the left, high up on the hill, was the Castle: below, the twinkling lights of the town. On his right the meadows stretched for less than a mile, before the woodland began again. He turned to the right, and made his way across the fields, towards the bluff and the little pond.

As though sensing something unnatural in the stumbling shape that came so blindly among them, the sheep scattered with little cries of alarm, the old bellwether trotting away far in advance of his flock.

On went the Monster towards the little bluff. His mouth was working, although no sounds came from it but a low gurgling: and his hands were waving like a penguin's flippers.

The shepherdess was patting a sheep that had thrust its muzzle against her soft thigh.

She sighed: it was so peaceful. The town going to sleep below, the nightingale beginning his song in woods behind her ... Oh! She stretched her arms above her head, and glanced around.

Then she screamed ... and screamed ... and screamed again. She was looking only at the Monster as she rent the air with her shrieks, so that she stepped back from the bluff: the grass gave way beneath her feet on the very edge of the small cliff.

There was a shriek louder even than the others, and she plunged into the pool below.

The dark shape above watched her fall: watched her wild efforts as she struck out in the icy water.

It stood there chuckling for a long second. Then it leaped out, and in a moment it had joined the girl below.

She was fighting now: fighting drowning, and something worse than drowning.

And now those steel arms had her tightly grasped: she struck at the white, glistening face with her tiny clenched fists. Struck, wildly, blindly; bruising it—gashing it with her nails.

And still that grasp did not relax, as she was borne towards the edge of the pool. ...

It was an unconscious girl that the Monster threw down on the grass at the water's edge.

He surveyed the supine form at his feet, and grunted. He stirred it with his boot and it did not move. Still grunting, he dropped on his knees beside the girl's body, and took one cold hand in his. He stroked her face, an unknown emotion sending a pleasant warmth through his body.

The girl opened her eyes, uncomprehending. She blinked her eyes: and then, as she saw the face bending over her, she screamed again.

The Monster pawed her face, and the girl shrank back.

"Don't touch me!"

There was a growl, as the clumsy hand sought her face once more.

A scream: and this time, as though human reason were breaking beneath a burden of horror unbearable.

Two hunters who were passing through the woods stopped as they heard the scream.

"What was that, August?"

"I don't know, Heinrich. What did *you* think it was?"

"To me," said August, the younger of the two, "it wounded like a woman's cry."

Heinrich shook his head.

"A cat, I think. They sound very human."

"That's true," said the other, resuming his walk.

Then, clearly through the night air, came another shriek; and this time they could hear a girl's voice sobbing with horror.

"A woman, August, in trouble. Quick."

They turned and ran through the woods.

"Is you gun loaded, Heinrich? Mine isn't."

"Yes. . . . Oh, look! It's a woman . . . August, load quickly. As God's my judge, it's the Monster!"

The other man brought his gun to his shoulder, shouting to draw the Monster away from the girl. Both men could see that the creature had clapped his hand cross the girl's mouth: but her flailing arms and kicking legs told them that at least she was not dead.

What other injuries she might have sustained they did not dare consider.

August was busily loading his gun, emptying a dram of powder from his powder-horn into each barrel, and ramming the plugs feverishly down with his ramrod.

"Heinrich, my gun is loaded. I am the better shot. Can you draw him off while I shoot him. We don't want to get the girl," he shouted.

"Hi you, there! Get away from that young lady. All right, miss; help's coming!"

The Monster raised his head and turned his white face slowly around.

"Heinrich! Watch!"

The great form struggled to his feet.

"August! Now . . . there he is! Shoot. . . !"

The Monster had abandoned the girl. With arms outstretched, he stumbled blindly towards the two men.

"Shoot, August!"

But August had served his time in the Austrian war, and he remembered his old musketry sergeant's advice:

"Never shoot until you see the whites of their eyes."

There was a patch of moonlight which the Monster would have to cross; and August was waiting for that. He was coming nearer: nearer: nearer.

He was running now: right across the carpet of light.

Crack! Crack!

August gave him both barrels, and even in that uncertain light they saw the Monster's face twist with pain. There was a groan, and the stumbling figure swayed in its tracks: one hand grasping the other forearm.

"Wrist, I think," said August. "Bad luck! I wonder if it's worth it in this light?"

"August," said Heinrich, nervously, "why don't we go for help?"

"To the town, do you mean?"

"Yes . . . it's better, I think."

"All right," said the younger man, giving his companion a push. "You cut along to the town as quickly has you can. Tell the Burgomaster. Tell him, it's the Monster. Quick now!"

"And you, August?"

"I'm all right. I'll look after the girl. Here! give me your gun. . . ."

CHAPTER XI

THE PURSUIT

IT was just at the finish of his seventh tankard of lager that the Burgomaster heard a man running through the Market Place, shouting, and sending the echoes chasing each other among the dormer windows and carved finials of the twelve-century Rathaus.

"Who's that drunkard?" he asked, in his testy way.

But the door of the inn was flung open, and his question was answered.

"Burgomaster. . . ." the man panted, "he's in the woods!"

Already a crowd was gathered around the door, and excited voices were repeating the hunter's words.

"What is it now?" the Burgomaster demanded.

The man pointed in the direction of the hills.

"The Monster, sir! He's in the woods."

"Rubbish!"

"No sir," said the man, with a deadly earnestness that the Burgomaster could not shrug away. "My mate shot him: wounded him. . . ."

The hubbub was rising, and the Burgomaster could detect the rising tide of consternation that the hunter's words had unloosed. He realized that something more than words were expected of him now, if he were to maintain his prestige. He snapped out an order.

"Here, you! Get out the bloodhounds. Raise all the men you can. Women to be locked indoors, and to wait for me."

He pushed his way out of the tavern, into a Market Square that miraculously had already filled with people.

His was that kind of courage which is strongest in public, when the eyes of the world are on it.

He puffed out his cheeks, and twisted his moustaches.

"Monster, indeed! I'll show him. Follow me!"

He led the way through the town, the townsmen following at his heels, quite silent, and slipping into their houses as they passed, to get a gun, an axe, or a stick.

Behind him, the Burgomaster could hear snatches of conversation.

"Wonder how many he'll kill this time."

"He's not human. *We'll* never kill him . . . not with *these* things, anyhow."

"You're right, Carl! Only the sacred bullet will kill such as he. . . ."

"Baron Henry will have much to answer for. . . ."

"Bah! Baron Henry has nothing to do with it. . . ."

"Yes, Adolf, truly . . . I heard it to-day. It is a vampire; and only cutting off his head, and piercing his heart with an ash-stake will kill him. Look, I have a piece of garlic in my pocket for protection. . . ."

"And in your breath, too!"

Oh, these peasants! The Burgomaster halted his men just outside the town, and they waited for the dogs to be brought.

He made a little speech, exhorting them to bravery; and everybody clapped to keep up his own spirits.

"Now, men, remember that the honour of Frankenstein Town depends on you to-night. By obeying my orders, you can rid this world of a most unpleasant madman; and secure the safety of all of us."

There was a baying and helping. The dogs had arrived, in the charge of a gendarme.

"Good," said the Burgomaster, eyeing their slavering jaws, and rubbing his hands in profound satisfaction. "*Now* let him escape!"

He turned to the hunter Heinrich, who stood at his side.

"Lead on," he ordered; and the little army marched towards the woods.

"Do you think we'll have to go far?" the Burgomaster asked Heinrich.

"I don't think so. My friend will have kept an eye on him."

"Oh, ah, um . . . yes, your friend . . . I'd forgotten him."

"He's a good marksman," said Heinrich. "He's already wounded him."

"Badly?" the Burgomaster asked, with some show of interest.

"I couldn't see. I don't think so."

"Pity." He pursed his lips. "This fellow seems to have as many lives as a cat. But never mind; we'll capture him, or kill him, to-night."

"Pray God we do," said a man behind them. "I for one, shan't sleep easy in my bed, until I know he's safe and sound."

"Never fear," said the Burgomaster, with a pompous assurance that, in truth, he was far from feeling. "Never fear. . . ."

67

So they passed on their way: up the mountain path. Through pine woods they went: their feet making no sound on the soft carpet of pine needles: the dogs silent, the muzzles sniffing the ground: the men hushed, as they drew near to their quarry.

"It was near here," Heinrich whispered.

"Just here?"

"No . . . beyond this. There's an open space where the road runs under a cliff. The some more woods, and after that some meadows. It was in the meadows, that August shot him.

They came out of the woods, and hurried along the mountain road. The dogs were sniffing the air, baying: and the men were seeing to the priming of their muskets and pistols.

"Not far now," said Heinrich to the company.

His words carried in the still night air. They carried, indeed, to a point where the cliff overlooked the road. And here a gaunt form crouched, watching with dull, unwinking eyes, the procession of men and dogs.

He saw them emerge from the wood, and disappear under the cliff, out of sight.

He judged the time when they should be directly underneath.

Then he shouted, standing erect: his tall body etched against the full moon.

"There he is!" the Burgomaster shouted. "After him!"

He swept forward, as his men pressed on. But above, the Monster, seeing the harrying pursuers, suddenly exerted his tremendous strength against a rock that was perched precariously on the very edge of the cliff.

He pushed, and the rock swayed.

Again; and with a dull roar, the huge mass broke away; crashing down on to the road below.

It splintered on the mountain path, crushing men and dogs, and sending up a mighty cloud of blood and dust.

For several seconds the Burgomaster and his companions stood as though turned to stone: too shocked by this sudden catastrophe to make a movement.

Then the Monster shouted once again from above, and the spell was broken.

"Stay behind, some of you, and look after the wounded, the rest follow me!"

The dashed along the mountain road. The moonlight was strong, and in its glare they could see the Monster standing on the peak overlooking the spot from which rose the mingled groans and curses of the injured men.

"We can cut him off," a man panted, "provided he doesn't double back on us."

"Then hurry, all of you!" the Burgomaster shouted: and panting and puffing, the crowd ran quickly up the road, with many anxious glances at the cliff edge above.

Heinrich said to the Burgomaster as he ran,

"I think when we're captured the Monster, I'll go and look for my friend . . . I can't think how we can have missed him. . . ."

The Chief Citizen shook his head and groaned.

"He's the hardest thing to kill *I've* ever struck . . . but look! look! There he is! Men, after him!"

They had come to the top of the rise, and were now on the small plateau that overlooked the road. The Monster was still standing where he had been when they had seen him from below; shouting and capering as the rock had gone crashing down.

He seemed to have heard the cries of his pursuers, but he was still gazing down at the mangled remains beneath.

"Slip the hounds," said the Burgomaster, hardly daring to believe that it was the Monster himself who stood less than fifty yards away: who had made no attempt since his murderous assault from the cliff, to elude capture.

"He can't have heard us," Heinrich muttered.

"I don't like the look of this," said an old farmer. "Looks to me as though there's some trap. . . ."

"Trap!" scoffed another. "He simply knows he doesn't stand a chance; that he'd better come quietly."

But the next minute showed the last speaker in error. The hounds had slipped their leash, and had bounded forward to where the Monster was facing the slowly advancing crowd. The moonlight glittered on knives and swords, and the polished points of pitchforks. It danced on the polished wood of thorn clubs, and the broad, flat blades of butchers' cleavers.

Urged on by the shrill cries behind, the dogs advanced on the towering form, from whose open mouth a dreadful sort of growling was coming. The Monster's hands were waving in the aimless fashion of a child's, who cries for temper. But the eyes were no eyes of a child: so deadly cold were they, so glittering, so merciless, so filled with a cold, passionless, purposeful, cruelty.

Men shuddered, as every detail of that monstrous frame stood out clearly in the light of the moon. More than one crossed himself, and whispered a prayer, as the band advanced; deploying, so as to hem the quarry in.

Then the voice of the Burgomaster was heard.

"Look at the dogs!"

His nerves must have been strained to snapping-point. For it was a quite unnecessary remark. Everybody had seen the dogs, seen them bound forward, mouths open, jaws slavering. Then, stopping dead, as though they had dashed into some invisible barrier.

That everybody had seen and seen, too, how the dogs, snarling and whining, had tumbled over each other in their efforts to escape from the dread presence.

That spectacle released a wave of superstitious fear which threatened to overwhelm the fast disappearing courage of the Mayor and his men. The hounds had sought the protection of the master's legs, and from here they were whining and snarling, until it seemed that their ululation must be heard over the whole barony.

It was Heinrich who saved the day. As he gazed at the clumsy, rocking body, he thought suddenly of young August. He shouted: "Men, where's your courage? Think of your wives and children! Think of little Maria Kramer, whom this fiend strangled to death!"

His words were enough. Ashamed of their momentary hesitation, the men swept forward, shouting and yelling, and brandishing their motley weapons. The Burgomaster leaned up against a tree, mopping his head with a bandanna handkerchief. He saw the advance, heard the cries of attacked and attackers, the yelping of the dogs, the oaths of men whose heads and legs found contact with the Monster's flailing limbs. There were the sounds of many blows; and a deal of panting, and choking, and crying out.

And at last the welcome shout: "We've got him!"

CHAPTER XII

THE CAPTURE

THE Burgomaster pushed his way through the crowd, elbowing the men aside, until he stood before the gaunt form of the captured man. One eye was closed, the head was cut in a dozen places. One hand was red with blood, which looked black in the moonlight.

"Are you holding him tight?"

"Yes, your Honour!"

"Good, bind him securely. I don't want anything slipshod!"

He stood over the Monster, while two men trussed him to the long trunk of a dead sapling, which was lying there.

"Tightly now! Two men, run down to the village. Tell them all's well, and bring back the first wagon you can find!"

He rubbed his hands in high satisfaction.

"A good night's work, gentlemen. I'll see you're not forgotten for this. Hello! what's this? Who cut his hand?"

"My friend did it," said Heinrich. "He shot him."

"Pity he didn't make a job of it! said someone in the crowd.

"I'll go and look for him, your Honour."

"Yes, yes . . . do! I hope that wagon won't be long. . . ."

In the distance they could hear shouting and the noise of a mob. It was coming from the direction of the town.

"What can that be?" the Burgomaster wondered.

"Well, grinned the little grocer who had been reprimanded in the Inn. "You don't think that the wagon's coming back without attendants, do you? If you want my opinion, the whole of Frankenstein that can walk is coming up."

"I do not want your opinion, my good man," the Burgomaster said pompously, "but you may be right."

He was, very nearly. The two messengers had commandeered a

hay-wain from the Market Place, and they were perched by the side of the driver, who was cracking his whip, as though he were going to a hiring-fair. And behind them, and preceding them, and on either side of them, was such a concourse of people, laughing and dancing, as made the Burgomaster gasp.

The grocer grinned at his astonishment.

"Didn't I tell your Honour that they'd bring the whole of Frankenstein with 'em?"

(Objectionable man! the Burgomaster thought. It's the effect of this damnable French revolution. . . .)

But openly he said, amiably enough, "Yes, no wonder they're excited! I'll tell them I've got the Monster safe and sound!"

The crowd came up with the rumbling wagon. From the cliff, the captors waved to the procession far below, and the townspeople answered with shouts.

From the very peak where the Monster had sent the rocks tumbling down, the Burgomaster called to his two messengers, "Tell the waggoners to mind the rock lying in the road. And you women, there: attend to the injured men!"

The procession rounded the cliff, and came up to the plateau.

"Have you really got him?" "String him up!" "Let's shoot him." A hundred different cries deafened the Burgomaster.

He held up his hand for silence.

"Pray silence, good people of Frankenstein! Your Burgomaster and some of your fellow townspeople have captured the madman you call the Monster. We have bound him securely, and he will now be taken to the prison-house: there to await his proper trial for murder and riotous behaviour."

A voice, a familiar voice, asked: "Have you got him? That's what I want to know. Have you got him?"

The Burgomaster frowned, making little clicking noises with his tongue.

"Of course we've got him, my good woman."

"And a good job too," said Minnie. "Mind he don't get loose again! He might do some damage, and hurt somebody. . . !"

The Burgomaster paid no attention to this laborious sarcasm. He shrugged his shoulders contemptuously, and shouted, "Bring the Monster down here, if he's securely tied."

A voice said. "We've got him, all right!

"Then bring him along."

They saw men heave the sapling upright, with its struggling burden bound to it with so many ropes, that it looked like a corpse in its cerecloths. They held it erect, while others pelted the gaunt, writhing figure, with mud and stones. Minnie yelled delight: but there was something about the scene which caught the Burgomaster's heart. It was too much like torturing an animal, to see the uncomprehending, dull agony on that white scarred face.

He said abruptly: "Leave him alone! Bring him down here. It's nearly dawn, and I want to get to my bed!"

Minnie said, "Need any help there? I'll bind him!"

The Burgomaster asked, wonderingly, "Don't you *ever* go to bed?"

"Sometimes! When there's no Monsters about."

"Don't they have any work for you up at the Castle?"

"A bit. . . ." She tossed her head. "I'm the Baroness' lady's maid. I don't have no common work to do.:

"Really?" he smiled. "And what does the Baroness think of all this?"

"She's not very pleased, of course."

"Naturally . . . as Baron Henry is dead."

"Oh, no! He's not. . . ."

Incredulously: "He's not. . . ? But I saw. . . ."

"Well," said Minnie, glad to have astonished him with her news, "he's not dead. And what's more, it was me who discovered he wasn't. Otherwise," she added gravely, "he might have been buried, and no one a penny wiser. . . ."

"You mean . . . he's . . . he's recovered. . . ?"

"I do. Of course," she sucked in her lower lip, after the manner of her tribe all over the world; "he ain't what you'd call hale and hearty. But he ain't *dead.*"

The Burgomaster shook his head in a dull wonder. Coming on top of all the excitement of this night, he was as yet unable to assimilate the information. All he could do was to repeat in a bewildered way: "But I saw him fall from the mill . . . I saw him with my own eyes. . . ."

"I *know,*" said the woman, "But these Frankensteins have got heads as hard as their hearts. . . ."

"They must have," the Burgomaster said curtly. He turned to the men who were bearing the pole-slung Monster across their shoulders.

"All right, man. Pitch him into the wagon. That's right. Up she goes. . . ."

There was a yell as the body shot through the air, to land with a thud in the wagon.

"Lord, that was a crack!"

"Bah! There's some straw there . . . who cares, anyway?"

A few stones followed the Monster into the cart, and then the driver cracked his whip above the lumbering drays.

The cart moved off and, followed by the cheering crowd, Frankenstein's creature was brought back to the town which so lately had shuddered at the very mention of his name.

CHAPTER XIII

DOCTOR PRETORIUS IS OPTIMISTIC

AT about the time when Minnie was describing Henry's miraculous recovery to the Burgomaster, the subject of their conversation was preparing
to leave his host.

It was now almost day, and the grey first light had crept in through
the chinks in the closed shutters, dimming the lamps and chilling the
atmosphere of that never very comfortable room, in which they sat.

Henry's apprehension had vanished in the face of an ever-increasing
interest that was rapidly mounting to fanaticism. Minnie had referred in
her coarse way to the hard hearts of the Frankensteins; but that was not
really true. They were hard certainly, when occasion demanded firmness of
purpose; but the quality that most impressed one in studying the character
of this ancient and remarkable family, was that of an utterly inflexible *will*.

Whatever they set their hands to do, those Frankensteins, they truly
did it with all their might: and no consideration of person, or place, or
circumstance, had the least power to turn them from the prosecution of
that adventure on which they were embarked.

The Doctor was no fool, and besides, he was a man many years older
than the young Baron Frankenstein. His psychology was sound, whatever
his morality; and he was above all things what we call "a man of the world."

So he had not cajoled Henry into accepting the partnership. Neither had he threatened him (when he might so easily have done so).
No, he had simply and cunningly, worked on the young man's vanity;
deferring to him; asking, not that he come as a pupil or assistant, but
that the Doctor be allowed, as a favour, to work with him. Indeed, so

75

skillfully had Pretorius set about his business, that as the dawn pierced the shutters, and carpeted the dirty boards with something greyer than their dust, Henry had almost come to believe that it was he, and not the Doctor, who had first suggested this monstrous making of the dead-in-life.

"A woman, Henry! Now that would be *really* interesting. . . ."

Henry's eyes lit up; and watching him, the Doctor smiled.

In the old days it had seemed that there would be no more apt a pupil than Henry Frankenstein, but . . . well, things had turned out badly. There had been that scandal at the University and the Doctor had had to lie low for a bit. Then he had lost touch with his pupil, and what with one thing and another, contact had been broken.

They had gone on with their work, indeed, but in different ways, and without collaboration. Pretorius sighed as he thought of the errors that might have been avoided, the redundant work saved, had they been free to compare notes, to use each other's experience.

Neither was growing any younger, and every moment was precious in such an undertaking as that upon which the minds of both were set.

Yet, it was no good drying over spilt milk. What was done was done. There were still (pray God!) many years ahead, and in that time, who knew what might not be accomplished?

That was why he had taken his courage into his hands, and demanded to speak to Henry. He had been among those who had seen the young man cast headlong from the flaming mill. He had seen his inert body gathered up, and laid reverently upon the bier, and he had been among those who had waited in the Castle yard before the great door, until the Baroness Elizabeth should receive the dead body of her lover.

But, alone among those who stood bareheaded around the bier, he had a doctor's knowledge; and there was something about the appearance of the body which, to his sharp eyes, was inconsistent with death. And he had thought to do what had occurred to no one else of all that mournful company. He moved up to the bier, and furtively touched a wrist with his sensitive fingers. All eyes had been fixed on the door, and no one had seen his action, but had anyone been looking they would have been surprised to see the Doctor smiling.

Well, he had taken his courage in his hands, and now, having played his cards well indeed, he had gained a partner whose knowledge would be of inestimable value, and who strong purpose would render him at once energetic and trustworthy.

Dr. Pretorius tired though he was, was conscious of a deep happiness as he reflected on his good night's work.

"Then . . . it is arranged?" he asked Henry, and the young man nodded, yawning involuntarily.

"I'm sorry," he said. "I must be tired. After all," he smiled, "I've had a very exciting night."

"Of course," the Doctor said courteously. "A little more gin before you go? No? Very well, I'll see you to the door."

He took a lamp from the table, and led the way to the top of the stairs.

"Mind how you go. There's a board out on the fifth one down."

Henry manœuvred the hole, and the Doctor followed him. As they stood in the open doorway, Henry put out his hand.

"Goodbye, Herr Professor. Here is my hand on our bargain. Goodbye."

He roused the sleepy coachman, and with a jingling of harness and cracking whip, the carriage started for Castle Frankenstein.

The Doctor watched the equipage until it had rounded the corner of the street. It was a thoughtful man who turned slowly into the house, and walked upstairs, into a study whose table was littered with dirty cups and glasses, and whose air was rank with stale tobacco-smoke.

He threw open the windows and let the cool morning air blow upon his face. From the direction of the Market Place he heard the sounds of shouting and cheering, and wondered vaguely what they could be cheering at this time of the morning. He supposed the news of Henry's recovery must have been broadcast. He knew that sycophant Burgomaster would not lose an opportunity of displaying his loyalty to the ruling family.

Then he smiled sardonically, as he reflected that it was Henry who was responsible for the terrible events of the past few weeks. What would their loyalty be worth if they knew that?

Smiling still, he shrugged his shoulders, and walked over to the bell pull. He tugged at the rope, setting a bell jangling far below. Then the shuffling footsteps sounded in the hall, on the stairs, and presently Franz stood in the room, blinking, and rubbing the sleep from his bleary eyes with his clenched fists.

The Doctor motioned to the hunchback to shut the door behind him. For a few moments he did not speak, walking up and down the room with his hands clasped behind his back.

Then: "Franz, do you know who that was with me to-night?"

"You told me, Master. The young Baron Frankenstein."

"Oh, did I? Yes, of course, I remember. Well . . now, listen Franz."

The sullen voice said: "I'm listening," and the Doctor smiled to hear the resentment in those sullen tones. He raised his eyebrows as he surveyed his servant from head to foot, running his eyes insolently over every limb and feature of that malformed and contorted body.

"Now listen, Franz, carefully, even if you *were* listening before. . . ." He paused, then resumed in a softer voice, "I know you hate me, Franz . . . Oh, don't look so surprised and resentful. Of *course,* you hate me. And I don't blame you. *I* certainly should feel the same, in your position. I'm not a kind man, Franz, I'm not even a fair man, but at least I'm an understanding man.

"And that enables me to sympathize with you, even when I see your fingers working spasmodically (do you know that word, Franz?) and how that you're itching to strangle me."

He laughed lightly.

"And I can sympathize too, Franz, with your chagrin when, after having searched every nook and cranny of this place, you fail to find a trace of that confession you so foolishly signed in a moment of mental stress. Dear me! he sighed, *"you were* overwrought that night . . . well, well, *nemo mortalium omnibus horis sapit,* Franz: which means in German, that it's only rabbits who sleep with one eye open. . . .

"But, Franz, I didn't call you up to tell you this. Curiously enough, in the last few hours, a wave of quite unwonted tenderness towards my fellow creatures has swept over me. I may be because things are turning out even better than I hoped, or it may be because—I'm just growing old.

"No matter, I've softened: let's face it. And it came to me, that while you have been obedient and willing from quite the most appalling motives, still the fact remains that you have been one of the best, and certainly one of the cheapest . . . hee, hee! . . . servants I have ever had.

"Do you ever read the Good Book, Franz? No? Tut, tut! You should, you know. It says there, that the labourer is worthy of his hire. I agree.

"Now, listen carefully, Franz. . . ." The bantering tone was gone, and Dr. Pretorius was in deadly earnest. His strange green eyes narrowed as he said, slowly and deliberately, "the young Baron Frankenstein and I are engaged on an experiment, which, if successful, will ensure us worldwide recognition as scientists. But . . . the Baron is not altogether to be trusted, Franz. It pains me to say it, but it is true. I am therefore going to let you help me.

"I shall need certain things, Franz, for my experiments, about which the Baron knows nothing. I think," he whispered, with a leering grin, impossible to describe, *"that you understand?"*

The unemotional voice said: "I understand, Herr Doktor. . . ."

"Good. Nothing can go wrong. We have the protection of the Freiherr. And if successful, Franz . . . I shall not need you any longer. I will make you," he said grandiloquently, "a present of your liberty. . . and no doubt the Baron, if I ask it, will make some little financial provision for your future. So be good, Franz, and you may yet be the Burgomaster of Nüremberg! Hee, hee. . . ! And now bring me my beaver and cloak. I'm going to see what they are all shouting about.

CHAPTER XIV

THE BURGOMASTER'S PRESTIGE IS EVEN FURTHER ENHANCED

THE dawn that saw the entry of the Monster into Frankenstein Town lived long in the memory of the inhabitants. Most of them, indeed, were gathered around the hay wain in which their captive was lying, bound to a tree trunk as tightly as rope (and lots of it) could bind him. The Monster's entry into Frankenstein was, indeed, more in the nature of a Midsummer carnival than anything else. It would have been hard for anyone unacquainted with the disturbing occurrences of the last few weeks to have understood that the prisoner entering the Market Place in so uncomfortable a fashion, was that figure of terror, at the very thought of whom the whole town had trembled in a panic fear.

But so adaptable is the human mind: so mercurial is it in its reactions to the manifold mutations of hope and anxiety; so ready is it to turn its back on distress, and usher in the millennium with the first stray sunbeams of spring; so apt, in short, to be as forgetful of yesterday, as it is to be deceived concerning the morrow; that it may well be understood that the people of Frankenstein no longer cringed and whimpered, but danced in an abandon of assurance that the Monster was among them once again.

Leading this imploring cavalcade was, of course, the Burgomaster. In the short distance from the cliff where the Monster had been captured, to the centre of the Town, an amiable self-deception had enabled him to persuade himself that almost single-handed he had overcome this public menace, and earned for himself and his descendants the undying glory of having rid the Barony (and, who knows, perhaps the whole Holy Roman Empire?) of the greatest menace to its peace since the *Vehmgericht* had been stamped out.

So he capered along at the head of this gallant company; his buff coat with its brass buttons open to show his scarlet, gold-corded waistcoat beneath, and the watch-chain swinging like a pendulum from the embroidered fob. He would have liked to wave his hat in the air; that beautiful new hat of Austrian velour with the quail's feathers, of which he was so proud. But, well, Burgomasters didn't wave their hats, except when Royalty of the Castle were present, and besides, the morning air was chilly for a bald head.

Dr. Pretorius came through one of the side streets that debouched into the Market Place, just as the unwieldly cortège halted in front of the statue of Maria Theresa.

The shouts were deafening, and what people were not gathered about the hay wain, were leaning from the windows, or standing in the doorways of the houses which lined the three sides of the Square.

"Dear me," the Doctor muttered, "I wonder what all this can be?"

He turned to a woman who, standing on tip-toe, was craning her neck in an endeavour to see over the heads of the dense crowd.

"Can I lift you up?" he smiled.

The woman looked up at his mocking face, half amused, half angry.

"Oh, go on . . . you saucy thing!"

"Tell me," says the Doctor. "What *is* all this how-de-do?"

She turned astonished eyes up to him; her mouth a wide O of wonder.

"Lordy! And where have you been that you don't know what's happened?"

"Where you should have been, my good woman: in my own house. . . . But tell me, since you seem to know. What *is* all this shouting and clamour?"

"The Monster. . . ."

"What about him?"

"He's *here!*"

"What's left of him, eh? That fire can't have left much."

She shook her head, craning it in order to miss nothing of the enthralling spectacle.

"No . . . he was alive . . . all the time. . . Well, look, you're taller . . . over there . . . see the pole?"

"I see a wagon: a hay wain. They're taking something out. The plague on my eyes! I can't see so far. . . ."

"Ah," she whispered, "he's tied up to a tree . . . he was captured in the woods after a terrible fight. They set the hounds on him, but . . . they wouldn't go near him. . . ."

"Why?"

For answer, she made the ancient sign of the thumb thrust between two fingers: a sign older than the roots of the hills; a sign of power more ancient than the oldest thing that is; the sign by which men may walk unmolested of the terror that walketh by night, and the pestilence that walketh by noontide. . . .

The Doctor nodded. Even he, for all his cynicism, felt a curious little shudder of apprehension as he saw that gesture. She saw the slight shiver, and nodded.

"It's cold here," she muttered, "but it's colder where they'll be sending him. . . ."

And now a full-throated roar shattered the limpid blue of the dawn.

"Look!" she chanted, "they're hoisting him out . . . oh! my, ain't he horrible?"

Pretorius saw a shape that bore but the faintest resemblance to a living man, raised by a dozen will hands, until it stood upright; bound to its wooden pillar; etched, a shape of grim darkness against the clear light of morning. There was something so helpless in the way the great, gaunt body hung there, supine, defeated; the eyes closed in the bruised, white, tormented face; that the mob was, of a sudden, stilled to silence.

The very fear that the Monster had once inspired, lent him a dignity which made itself felt, even by these simple, unimaginative people. Even in captivity; torn, wounded, defiled by pelted rubbish; he was yet greater than they.

Pretorius, looking up at the crucified figure, thought of the lumbering stupid strength of a bull that has been brought to bay by a pack of hounds.

He murmured: "Yes, Henry knew what he was about."

The woman looked up as he spoke.

"Eh? What was that?"

"Oh, nothing . . . Shall we move nearer?"

She followed close behind him, as he elbowed his way through the excited, doom-hungry mob. Nor, indeed, was there cause for his pushing, for the crowd fell aside to allow him passage, awed a little by a certain authority that was always the most noticeable thing about him.

So at last they stood together, not a dozen paces from where the little bantam turkey-cock of a Burgomaster was superintending the incarceration of the Monster. By his side, in all the glory of bullion epaulettes and plumed brass helmet, the Chief of Police was giving orders to two or three gendarmes, whose task it was to preserve a clear space around the wagon.

"All right, men," said the Burgomaster, "bring him down. Ah, come along! No need to be so finicky with him. He wasn't so finicky with little Maria Kramer!"

Approving growls from the crowd greeted this sally, and the Chief Citizen felt that his prestige would not suffer by this morning's work.

The men in the wagon let the end of the pole fall to the ground with a crash and the body on the beam jerked in its bonds. A moan burst from the blue lips, and the crowd laughed.

"He'll get worse than that," said the Burgomaster.

Now the men standing by the wagon picked up the end of the tree, and raised it to the level of their shoulders. Others took charge of the end still resting on the hay wain, and all together, they eased the beam off the cart.

"Make way, everybody! Make way!" the Burgomaster shouted.

The men moved off to the door of the prison, outside which the wagon had been halted.

"There endeth the first lesson," the Doctor sneered.

"Well," said his companion, "I should think it has been a lesson to all of us, especially to Baron Henry."

"Oh," said the Doctor, raising his eyebrows, "and what's *he* got to do with it?"

"Well," sullenly, "he started it."

"Did he now?" the Doctor murmured in benign sarcasm. "How interesting!" He nodded, and the woman scowled. Like all members of her class, she disliked and feared sarcasm.

"Well," she grumbled, "that's what they say."

"Oh, and what do they say?"

"Well . . . that . . . oh, well I couldn't quite get the hang of it. . . .But, anyway, he had something to do with it . . . that's all I know."

"And quite enough too," the Doctor murmured.

"I shouldn't say any more, if I were you." The woman turned apprehensive eyes on him. "They've long ears up at the Castle, and below-stairs gossip can't help you, in this world. . . ."

"No sir."

"That's a good woman. Ah, well, they're taking him into the dungeon, I suppose."

"That's right," the woman said, not quite recovered from her reprimand, and still a little shaken.

"They're going to put him in the garrotting chair . . . though of course they ain't going to kill him yet. Well, leastways, they are going to try him first."

"And kill him afterwards, eh?" the Doctor smiled.

"That's right, sir."

"Dear me," he said, "I wonder why they waste time trying him?"

"It's the law, sir."

"Of course, my dear. How silly of me to forget. . . ."

The Monster was by now out of sight. A crowd was collected about the door of the prison; but the gendarmes stood in front of it, with their carbines crossed; and all that was vouchsafed to the spectators was the sight of the porters carrying the Monster's body down the stone staircase, and the vivid imaginings of what would happen to him when he arrived in the dungeons.

But down in the dungeon, there was less of excitement, and more of anxiety.

Skillfully manœuvring the sharp corners of the old crypt's corridors, the men brought their bulky burden into the Execution Room.

Indifferently easing the weight from off their shoulders, they let the log fall, with a crash that brought a groan from the Monster's lips.

"There you are," said the Burgomaster. "Now be careful; if he shows any signs of fight, give him a hit on the head."

But the bruised, bewildered Monster showed no signs of fight; nor, indeed, of any interest in the world around him, as his captors carefully unbound his body from the tree-trunk and, pulling him along the stone floor, hoisted him into the great wooden chair in which the murderers died. They forced his head into the neckpiece, and bound the steel collar around his scarred throat.

His hands they manacled to the arms, and his feet to the legs of the chair.

"He'll do," said the Burgomaster. "But . . . well, hammer those manacles into the wood."

One of the men, a great brute of a fellow, took up a sledge-hammer; and with steady, even strokes beat the staples deeper and deeper into the worn oak of the chair. With each blow a groan escaped from the Monster's lips, and his heavy-hooded eyes opened: he gazed on his torturers with the dull ferocity of a helpless, baited animal.

"Come along," said the Burgomaster, "that will do; that's quite enough. Now come out, and bolt your doors. After all," he added, "we can't take all day for this.

He turned towards the door, and the men followed him.

On the step of the front door, Minnie was waiting; and in spite of the Burgomaster's frown, she shouted a cheerful:

"Well, got him all locked up safe and sound, your Honour?"

"Yes," he said tersely enough, "he's all right."

"Dear, dear," said Minnie. "I'd hate to wake up and find *him* under my bed at night. He's a nightmare in the daylight, he is."

Several people had crowded around the one small barred window which gave to the Monster's dungeon what small illumination it enjoyed. But not for long were they permitted to relish the spectacle which peering afforded them. The jailer caught two of the outermost spectators, and banged their heads together with a resounding crack. The others went without further example.

Only Minnie snapped:

"Mind your own business, and see that he doesn't get out! He's dangerous."

"I know he's dangerous," said the jailer contemptuously. "Why the devil don't you go back to the Castle, instead of interfering with everything you can stick your long nose into?"

"Well. . . !"

"Now, come, come," said the Burgomaster, "we've had enough squabbling for to-day." He turned to the crowd, hand upraised for silence.

"Good people, the Monster is now safe and sound. We have him secured in such a way as only a miracle could rescue; and now I want you all to go back to your homes."

The crowd began to scatter, realizing that the excitement was at last over: that there was nothing more to be seen.

The Burgomaster, wiping his forehead, said to the chief jailer:

"Well, now that's done, I can get back to more important duties."

"And leave us to ours," came *sotto voce* from a lesser jailer.

"Eh? What's that?"

"Good-night, sir," said the jailer with an apprehensive cough.

The Burgomaster buttoned up his buff coat.

"Monster, indeed! Tush . . . tush!"

CHAPTER XV

THE ESCAPE

NOW, there were no witnesses of the Monster's escape from the garrotting chair: so that it was never known exactly how that memorable feat was accomplished. There were naturally many who found in the escape additional evidence of the Monster's supernatural powers: but examination of the steel collar and manacles, afterwards, showed that the Monster had freed himself from his bonds by the exercise of a truly prodigious strength; but in no way that spoke of dematerialization, or any other trick, popularly ascribed to vampires.

All that was known of the escape came from two guards, who had been placed on sentry duty outside the door of the cell where the Monster was chained.

One guard, in describing the matter afterwards, told of hearing grunts and growls, louder and more purposeful than any he had heard before. He had walked along the corridor that led to the door of the cell. He had peered through the little barred window, just in time to see the Monster, already half-free, tug chain and staple from the floor, in one tremendous surge of strength.

He had the presence of mind to call his mate, just as the Monster pulled the other chain free.

Together, they had levelled their carbines through the grille, and fired; but it had been impossible to take aim; and, as it turned out afterwards, neither shot had taken effect.

The men had retreated down the corridor, shouting for help. In a second the noise of heavy blows resounded through the dungeons as the Monster beat at the panels of the door with a heavy iron bar which had been left in his cell.

"He's loose! He's loose!"

But the Monster, for all his enormous bulk, was faster than they. A heavy hand, powerful as a sledge-hammer, dashed them down, and he emerged from the front door into the Market Place, just as the Burgomaster was saying to a group of peasants,

"Now go to your homes. Just an escaped lunatic. Merely wanted somebody to handle it: that's all . . . Quite harmless. . .!"

There was a confused recollection in Frankenstein of a crowd suddenly turning tail in panic flight: of isolated and abortive attempts to wound or delay the Monster: of shots that never reached their mark: and guns that were torn out of their owners' grasps, and used to club the men who had fired them.

There was a dim remembrance of a gaunt figure flying through the Market Place: of a thousand eyes that followed, and a thousand bodies which shrank away. Of a child who was playing in the street: and whose tiny body, swinging in a monstrous arc, lay ominously still where it had fallen: and only the piercing shriek of the mother who had witnessed it broke the overpowering, enchanted silence.

What happened to the Monster between that morning and nightfall of the next day, no one knew. He left the town in that deadly silence: and though a multitude watched his unmolested departure, no one followed him along the high road that led to the woods and the mountains; to the cities under the hill, and the lands afar. . . .

The next news the people of Frankenstein had of the Monster, was from a gypsy and his wife: and from their tale it seemed probable that the Monster, on leaving the town, had made straight for the woods, there to lie in hiding until, at evening, he could creep forth in some immunity.

According to the gypsy, he and his wife had been sitting by their fire, talking of the events of the last few weeks. A joint was roasting over the fire; and the man, as he said himself, was snug and contented. But his wife, with the apprehension of her sex, was uneasy: fearful of every shadow, and starting at every noise.

She said to the child who was sitting at her side,

"Ramona, you stay close to me."

To her husband, she added,

"We'd better get away from these parts. It isn't safe."

"Why?" her husband asked contemptuously.

She ignored the contempt: returning his mocking gaze with her own dark steady gaze; her arm tight clasped around her child.

"I'm frightened . . . the Monster. . . ."

He shrugged away the danger.

"Aw! there's no peril. He's safe in jail; and they'll keep him there."

"I hope they do . . . but . . . well, I think we had better go somewhere else perhaps for a little while."

"Where to?" he asked sarcastically. "England, where they hang us if we stay more than a month: France, where one cannot live long enough even to be hanged, they're so stingy . . . ? No, Mother, we'll stay in our own country, where we know how to live and find our way about."

"All right," she murmured, only half convinced.

"Where's the pepper and salt?"

"It's in the wagon. I'll get it."

He turned, and walked over to the wagon, disappearing inside.

And it was then, apparently, that the woman first heard a snapping of twigs in the undergrowth, as though some heavy body were crashing through. There was a grunting noise. Then, in a few seconds her worst fears had been realized.

Into the circle of firelight, a gaunt, battered figure stumbled.

There was a scream from the woman and her child, and her husband came scrambling down the steps in his wagon.

But the Monster had not really been intent on bodily harm.

He was hungry; and as the man emerged from the wagon, the Monster grabbed at the meat on the spit.

But . . . the Monster was the Monster: and apparently it never occurred to the gypsy to spare his family at the expense of their dinner; or perhaps the terror which the very sight of the Monster inspired, had clouded his reason.

Whatever it was, he thought valour the better part of discretion. He snatched a blazing brand from the fire, and with this as a weapon, he attacked the Monster.

As the gypsy readily admitted afterwards, he was easily overpowered. The brand was snatched from his hand, and he himself thrown brutally aside. Half dazed by the fall, he saw the Monster make a grab at the meat, which, by now, had fallen on to the fire.

He had seen that great hand thrust into the flames: heard the squeal, the bellow of astonishment and pain, as the heat scorched that unnatural flesh. There had been a moaning sob, as the Monster clasped his hand to his breast: and with one bewildered look at the fire, had turned and fled once more into the woods.

CHAPTER XVI

"...AND GENTLENESS, IN HEARTS OF PEACE..."

IN a cottage set deep in the woods high above the town, lived a hermit. No one ever visited the little thatched hut where he lived alone; for it lay far off the main roads, and only a narrow track led to its door. Yet he was not entirely alone. The world had forgotten him, passed him by; even the blessing of sight had been taken from him. Yet he was, for all these things, not entirely alone. Years ago he had learnt that within us all lies an unplumbed mine, if not of happiness, then of content, which takes no heed of the busy hurrying world around, and which, if we but search for it, can give us back all that we seem to have lost. Certainly, on the face of the hermit was none of that worry, that frowning discontent, which too often marred the looks of the townsfolk. With his closed eyes adding an unthinkable repose to a look already serene, one might have said to see him, that he had risen above all the petty sins and longings which, by being mistaken for happiness, come between us and our peace.

As I say, he was not entirely alone. He had a companion; and never was wife or child more dearly loved than this old man's violin. Each night, the day's work done, the little hut swept and clean, the few humble crocks washed, and set on the old oak dresser, his loving, careful fingers would open the worn case, and take out the only thing which could share and lighten his life.

His eyes could not see, but his mind could picture, as clearly as though he were in the fullest possession of his sight, the firelight flickering on the mellow patina of the ancient varnish; see it dancing up the ebony stem, and curving around the twisted volutes of the head.

Each night for thirty years he had taken the old violin from its case, and laying his cheek softly against the swelling curves of its polished surface, drawn out with his delicate fingers the soft melodies which lay stored within. He lived too far off from the town, too deep within the unfrequented woods, to have heard the hubbub and the shouting which had been continuous since the evening before. Had he been able to see, the sky, lit with the glare from the burning mill, might have told him something was amiss; but blind and remote, he was blissfully unconscious of the terror and the hatred around him.

To him, the night was as peaceful as if two thousand miles, instead of a mere two, separated him from the world of men.

Yet, however far we may remove ourselves from our fellow creatures, an *absolute* isolation is the hardest thing to attain. Someone will find us.

It was as well for the old man that he knew nothing of the fearful events of the day; that he took his violin from its case, all unconscious of the forces that mad, insolent presumption had let loose upon the world.

He suspected nothing. Standing before the warm log fire, which by now had died down to a gentle glow, he played the dainty, simple tunes of a century ago: minuets, gavottes; pavanes; of Mozart, and Bach and Domenico Scarlatti; those, and older songs, remembered from his distant childhood, whose composers no one knew, so lost were their origins in the mists of antiquity.

He was playing a tender song of Rossini's as a tall, swaying shape came stumbling through the dense woods. Beneath its hurrying feet the dried twigs snapped and cracked, but the old man did not hear: and from out the open windows the soft music came floating.

The tall shape stiffened as it heard: and now, with more caution, it crept nearer; to peer at last through the open window.

For a minute it stood, its large hands on the sill, gazing into the small, humbly furnished room. It watched the hermit sitting before the fire; saw his staring, sightless eyes gaze vacantly ahead; observed the agile fingers trembling on the strings. And seeing all these things, the gaunt face smiled.

Yet, silently as the Monster had approached the little hut, some inner sense had warned the old man of a stranger's presence. With firm, unhesitating steps, he walked over to the door, and threw it open. A beam of light carpeted the trodden space in front of the door; and the Monster shrank back against the walls of the cottage.

The hermit called, into the night.

"Who's there?"

He stood there listening: but the only sounds were those of the wind as it made its gentle way through the trees. That, and a nightingale's sobbing nocturne.

"I was mistaken," he muttered; and turning into the room, closed the door behind him.

He drew a chair up to the fire, and sat down. Once more the violin was raised to his chin; once more the soft, fragrant notes came to soothe his heart into peace.

At the window was a face which he could not see: a face which smiled as it listened to the tender wailing of the violin.

It was a sound which never in its short, unnatural life had it heard before, but it was not less true of the Monster than was true of those other things which the poet Congreve mentions, when he says,

Music hath charms to soothe the savage breast,
To soften stones, or bend the knotted oak.

And the Monster was no more proof against its sweet influence than the softest heart that ever beat. He who had never known tenderness, or pity, or love for any beings; whose home was in the tomb, and whose cold heart pulsed with the unnatural passions of the dead, felt, for the first time, an unwonted calm within him; a cooling off of all that fierce hunger for pain and blood which, before, had driven his dull mind ever forward. So he stood, gazing through the open window at the calm sightless face before him, smiling, not indeed, for the first time in his life, but certainly for the first time at something pure, and sweet, and noble.

For some minutes he stood there; then, on a sudden resolve, he straightened himself and walked towards the door, his pursuers forgotten; the pain in his shattered arm, and burnt hand, forgotten. There was one desire only in his mind: to be near the music.

He threw open the door with one quick movement, growling in his old habit. The hermit turned his face towards the door.

"Who is it?"

There was no answer. The dull, tired face blinked suspiciously at the seated man. The staring eyes were fixed on the Monster. He did not know that they could not, never would, see the bloodstained hands; the scratched gaunt face.

He simply stood silent; so that the old man, with a puzzled half smile, waving his hand in a courteous gesture of hospitality, added,

"You're welcome, my friend, whoever you are."

91

There was a time when those great hands would have seized the throat before them; and with one quick blow, have dashed the head against the stone floor. But the power that long years of love and kindness had given to the saintly man before him, stayed his hand: some sense of a certain goodness in the world, dimly felt as yet, but every minute growing stronger and stronger, had touched the Monster's heart, and stayed his hand.

His feelings were instinctive: he did not know even, that he was behaving in a different manner from his usual behaviour. He simply did what many of you would be the happier for doing: he followed his heart.

And his heart told him to hold out his hands in the first gesture of friendliness that this strange product of a madman's mind had ever made.

As yet speech had not come to him. He was as a little child who has yet to learn how words are formed. But whereas a child learns from the loving lips of those around him, there had been no loving lips to teach the Monster the clear, expressive sounds of the German tongue. All he could do was to mumble, as he held out his bruised and bleeding hands.

The hermit rose, to face him; frowning a little that the stranger did not answer.

"Who are you?" he asked.

There was still no answer.

The old man came forward a few steps. Then:

"I think," he said, "that you must be a stranger to me." He paused, nodding his confirmation. "Of course, you're a stranger to me . . ."

He added pathetically:

"I cannot see you, you know . . . I cannot see anything. . . ."

He came forward again, as he said it.

"You must please excuse me . . . but . . . but . . . I'm blind."

He said it half hesitating, as though he seemed frightened that the stranger should misinterpret his excise as a self-compassionate angling for pity. But there was no answer. Only, from the doorway, came the strange mumbling. And across to the doorway went the old man, unhesitating and unafraid. Across to the tall, gaunt figure, before whom a whole town had turned and fled in terror.

Why the stranger remained so silent, the hermit had no idea; but to his pure soul no thought of fear had ever come to trouble it. Someone had opened his door, and to "the stranger within his gates" he offered nothing but the hand of friendship. He said gently:

"Come in, my friend. Close the door behind you." And as the stranger made no move: "No one will hurt you here." And at last the stranger answered. Not indeed, in words, but in a deep groan which wrung the old man's tender heart.

"Come in," he implored. "If you're in trouble . . . perhaps I can help you. Although," he added quickly, "you need not tell me about it if you don't want to."

If only he could have seen! If only he could have seen the tired, tortured face, as the stranger stood just within the doorway; trying to frame words with which to tell him all the things that needed so greatly to be said.

But he could not. So that he reached out his hand (if only the Burgomaster had been there!) and laid it on the Monster's shoulder. His tender hands asked the gentle question:

"What's the matter?"

There was only a growl for answer. . . .

A whole town had shuddered and fled to hear that growl.

But the hermit was of different make. He understood, although he could not see the face before him, that here was a fellow-creature in trouble.

"My poor friend," he said (the first time it was that anyone had called Frankenstein's Monster *that!*).

"My poor friend; come. . . ."

With a gentle force, he led the gaunt, stumbling form into the room and, laying his hands on the great shoulders, pushed it into a chair, while he took the seat beside it.

"Now sit down, my friend, and tell me all about yourself. Who are you?"

The stranger did not answer, but a great hand rested on the hermit's shoulder, just as he was about to rise. Sounds came from the man in front, but no sound that was like human speech. The hermit knew that it was a man: no woman was ever so tall or so heavily made.

And he began to think he understood why the stranger did not answer. After all, had not the good God, in his inscrutable wisdom, seen fit to take away from His servant the blessed gift of sight?

With a new tenderness in his voice he murmured:

"It is strange! Perhaps . . . perhaps you, too are afflicted. *I* cannot see, and *you* cannot speak." He asked gently, "Is that it?"

Still there was no speech. Only the uncouth sounds that he had heard before.

"Listen," said the hermit. "If you should understand what I'm saying—put your hand on my shoulder."

For one second he waited: then the hand rested on his shoulder.

"Good," he smiled, "*now* I understand."

"You stay here," he said, "and I'll get you some food. . . ."

As he felt his way across to the cupboard, his stick tapping on the stone floor, he murmured:

"We shall be friends . . . I know it . . ."

He took up a bowl of soup from the dresser, and came back to where the Monster was sitting.   Eager hands took the bowl from his grasp as he said:

"Oh, how often have I prayed God to send me a friend. It is very lonely here; and it has been a long time since any human being came into this hut."

In front of him he could hear the greedy lapping of the soup, could imagine the ravenous devouring of the bread; guessed well, how famished the stranger must have been. He said, with his gentle smile:

"I shall look after you, and you would comfort me. . . ."

"Yes," he nodded, "you would comfort me: I know that. . . ."

The empty bowl was thrust into his hands, and rising, the Hermit placed it carefully on the little table.

He came back to where his visitor was sitting, and laid gentle hands on his shoulders, motioning him to rise.

Obediently, the great figure rose stumblingly to its feet; and taking it by the arm, the Hermit led it to the pallet on which he was wont to rest.

"Now you must lie down, and go to sleep," he said.

He was blind: otherwise he would not have failed to see the gratitude that was so clearly marked on the face before him.

He rested his hands on the gaunt shoulders, and, with a gentle pressure, forced him to lie down: though, in truth, it needed no coaxing.

Now the Monster was lying on the Hermit's bed; and that kindly man had taken one of the bloodstained hands in his.

"Yes, yes . . . now you listen. . . ."

There was silence. Then the clear voice raised in prayer: the clear voice in which a sob of gratitude trembled.

"Our Father . . . I thank Thee, that in Thine exceeding mercy, Thou hast vouchsafed to take pity on my great loneliness . . ." He paused, stroking the hand of his uncomprehending, but grateful guest, before he resumed, with a sigh. "And now, out of the night, Thou hast brought two of they lonely children together . . . and," softly, "sent me a friend, to be a light to mine eyes, and a comfort in time of trouble." He added, gently reverent: "Amen. . . ."

So for some seconds he sat there in silence, revolving many memories until, at last, as the deep measured breathing told him that the other slept, his head sank down upon the bed; and he wept. . . .

And then, when his soft sobs were shaking the bed, a curious thing happened.

Of a sudden, a great hand rested on the Hermit's shoulder, reassuring him with its clumsy caress: while to his ears came the sound of weeping.

The Hermit smiled through his tears.

"Oh, my friend," he said, patting the rough hand that rested in rude affectionateness on his shoulder.

"Weep not for me. It is for happiness, and not for sorrow, that I weep. And if," he murmured musingly, "there be something of sorrow in my weeping, it is no more than regret for the lost years."

He sighed deeply.

"And now, my friend, sleep. . . ."

Soft fingers: the tender touch of a blind musician, closed the dull eyes. And the Monster slept, in the dreamless and unstirring slumber of childhood innocence.

Michael Egremont

CHAPTER XVII

THE PURSUIT CONTINUES

IT was hours later that the Hermit's guest awoke. The day had not yet broken, but the eastern sky had paled to the pearl of that hour which the Persians call "the false dawn" : the hour before sunrise.

Already in that little hut the darkness of night had given way to the indeterminate half-light of approaching day. Objects were faintly visible: the old carved armoire; the dull red glow where the fire had died down; the black mass of the bed on which the stranger slept; now a stranger no longer, the Hermit murmured to himself smiling.

He had not slept: the excitement of the night had banished all of sleep: and besides, it was over a sick man that he was watching. His gentle, sensitive fingers had discovered the gunshot wound on his friend's wrist. He had bathed it, and bound it up: but he knew that fever not infrequently followed such wounds. And attentively he had listened for any signs of acceleration in the even breathing, and occasional snores, that came from the bed.

The passing hours had quietened his apprehension somewhat. But sleep had not followed the calming of his fears.

So by the open window he had sat, listening to the sounds of the world waking around him: the faint, insecure chirrups of the birds: the stirrings of the little woodland creatures: the far-off call of a goatherd or milkmaid.

Through the open casement, a gentle breeze came to cool his brow: and over the mountain, though he could not see it, the pearl of the "false dawn" was slowly giving way to the blazing splendour of the true dawn.

"... the dawn
The hour the lilies open on the lawn,
The hour the grey wings pass beyond the
mountains,

96

The hour of silence, when we hear the
    fountains,
The hour that dreams are brighter and winds
    colder,
The hour that young love wakes on a white
    shoulder. . . ."

In the little plantation attached to the cottage, hens were kept. With the first beam of day, came a loud clucking.

It was this that awakened the Monster.

He stretched his arms: peered suspiciously about him: but as his eyes fell on the calm figure sitting by the open window, the remembrance of the past night came to him and he smiled.

He growled, but not in anger, and the Hermit called,

"Are you awake, my friend?"

He rose from his chair, and went across to the pallet. As he drew near, a hand caught his, and pressed it to a round cheek. The Hermit smiled, and smoothed the scarred forehead, wondering a little at the metal clips which bound the skull together, but saying nothing of his thoughts.

"You're awake then? Good! Then let us have some breakfast."

He walked across to the fire and held his hand over the dying embers to determine the warmth of it. Then, carefully adding a few chips of dry wood, he built it up into a modest blaze.

When it was to his satisfaction, he hung an old blackened kettle over it, and poked the fire into a more energetic condition.

"Well," he said cheerfully, "breakfast won't be long now."

There was a growl from the bed.

"Breakfast," he repeated good-humouredly.

"Don't you know the word. Say . . . 'Breakfast.' "

There was silence, then:

"Break . . . fast. . . ."

"Good!" he laughed.

The Monster chuckled, and repeated,

"Break-fast: break-fast: break-fast. . . ."

"Excellent," said the Hermit. "I thought at first that the blessed gift of speech was denied to you entirely. Now I praise God, that, by patience, I may yet open to you still another means of enjoying our companionship."

"Compan-ion-ship," the Monster repeated slowly.

97

"Ah, my dear friend," said the Hermit, with tears running down his cheeks, "you do not know what your coming has meant to me. . . . But see, the water is boiling. You like coffee?"

"Coff---ee."

"Ah, I see you do."

His deft fingers measured out the coffee beans into the mill: a few sharp turns, and he poured the drawer-full of ground coffee into the warmed pot. Next the water, hissing hot, followed; and the coffee-pot was stood at the back of the hob.

"Five minutes, and we breakfast," the Hermit announced.

He walked over to the bed, and with gentle pressure, bid the recumbent figure rise. The docile Monster was led to the table, and bidden to take a chair.

"Now," said the Hermit, picking up the bread, "we'll have our lesson. Remember—this is bread."

He held the loaf out, and the Monster reached across the table to take it.

"Bread," he repeated.

"And this," said the Hermit, pouring the hot liquid from the cup, and adding the coarse brown-molasses, "is coffee."

"Yes. It is good. Drink it."

The Monster sniffed at the steaming beverage, and began gingerly to drink, as the Hermit was already doing.

"Good," he said. "Coffee . . . good!"

He smiled, pleased with himself for having progressed so far on the road to learning. He raised the cup to his lips, and this time he did not put it down until it was finished.

"Good," he said.

The Hermit laughed.

"I'm glad you like it here. We are friends, you and I." He held out his hand and the Monster took it is his great rough paw.

"Friends," he chuckled. "Good . . . good!"

The Hermit rose and went across to the cupboard, returning with a flat wooden box, which he opened and laid upon the table.

"Now for a smoke," he said, taking a cigar from the box.

There was no answer, so he asked:

"You don't mind if I smoke, do you? Finish your breakfast, and then join me in a cigar."

He leant back, and drew a burning twig from the fire, holding it, with unerring judgement born of long practice, to the end of the Havana.

But now, from across the table came a growling that even to the Hermit's ears, was implicit with fear and anger.

The great hands waved in the air, and the great head shook.

The Hermit laughed, misunderstanding the cause of his guest's alarm.

"Oh, don't worry. I'm not on fire. See!" He took the cigar out of his mouth, and proffered it to the Monster.

But now the growls redoubled in fury.

The Hermit shrugged, and took another cigar from the box. He lit it, and handed it across the table.

"Take it," he said: and as if he could see the nervous gesture with which the Monster refused.

"No-no-no, this is good. Smoke. You try."

He put his own cigar into his mouth, puffing hard and expelling the smoke with every manifestation of pleasure. Cautiously, the Monster took the cigar from his fingers, and, still watching him closely, put the end gingerly into his mouth. He puffed: the end glowed, and the tobacco crackled: the fragrant smoke shone blue in the early morning sunlight.

He laughed, and the Hermit laughed to hear him.

"Good?"

"Good! Good—good—good!"

From across the table, a hoarse voice said,

"Alone: bad! Friends: good!"

He repeated, as though well pleased with his remark:

"Friends . . . good . . ."

"Excellent! And now, come here!"

He rose, and picked up a billet of wood from a pile of logs.

"And what is this?"

There was a growl for answer.

"This is wood . . . for the fire."

"Wood. . . ."

There was a laugh.

"And this is fire. . . ."

"Gr-rr-rh. . . ."

"No, no my friend! Do not be afraid: fire is good." He felt the arm he was holding, stiffen, and the great body draw back.

"Fire," said the Monster, "fire no good!"

The Hermit shook his head. Softly, he said, as though he were explaining to a child:

"Listen, my friend! There is good, and there is bad . . . in everything. Fire, properly used, is man's best friend: abused, it can be his greatest foe. . . ."

Now, whether his guest understood this little dissertation, he never knew: for a violin was suddenly thrust into his hands: and he found himself asking:

"Music?"

He caught up the bow, and drew it with a flourish across the strings.

"Sit down, my friend. Your body may be imperfect: but I can see that God hath given thee a soul. . . ."

He asked, with a wistful smile:

"And what would you like: a gavotte: a minuet: a pavane? Light; gay? Or something melancholy, yet sweet?"

"Good . . . good!"

"Ah, my friend," the Hermit replied, with a short, half-mocking laugh, "all music is good. Probably." he mused, "it is the only truly good thing there is; though even music has been bent to serve the ends of evil men. But I asked what I should play for you."

"Music . . . good," said his guest.

"I see . . . it matters not. Very well. . . ."

His fingers trembled on the volute of his violin: the wrist of his other hand rested in a preliminary vibration about the bridge: perched there, with the light, evanescent touch of a butterfly. A deep breath, a moment's hesitation; then the bow swept across in one clean gesture, as strong, as clear, as uncompromising, as the sweep of a sword.

The Monster clapped his hands: though the wound on his forearm made him wince.

"Good . . . *good. . .!*"

It was a little dance, that told sweetly of dewy meadows in dawn. It was sweet, and simple: with the sweetness of clear honey distilled in the cups of flowers: simple with the simplicity of life untouched of cities or the deceits of civilization. The tune was an old one, something that the composer had remembered from early childhood, when he had followed the rosy-cheeked maid with his milking-stool; had walked among the browsing kine, wetting his feet in the morning damp, while the sun came slowly up, casting the long shadows of the hills across a boy's naked feet.

The Monster's eyes were closed as he listened. What thoughts were passing through that gaunt head, one can never know; but certainly they were thoughts of peace. The tired, bewildered soul had been lulled into calm, for the first time in its short life.

And resting as peacefully as a child was the Monster at whose name men trembled, when—the hunters, Heinrich and August, had knocked at the door.

Since the early morning they had been scouring the woods, partly in search of the Monster, but in reality in the hopes of finding the road to the town.

Heinrich, as the reader knows, had been worried about his friend August. The fact that the Monster was at large and unharmed, seemed to point to some accident to August. For the younger man had been left on guard.

Immediately the capture of the Monster had been accomplished, Heinrich had slipped off to search for August. He remembered the spot by the little waterfall. The wood was fairly well-known to him, and the finding of August (provided that he had remained where Heinrich had left him, which he doubted) seemed an easy enough matter.

Full of apprehension, the older man had traversed the wood, starting at every noise, and bending down to examine every log or fallen tree-trunk that looked, in the dim light, like the prostrate body of a man.

His fears had been amply justified when, at last, he did find August. For he was fallen just as Heinrich had pictured him in his fevered imagination.

The young man was lying just at the edge of the wood where he had been left. His face was turned upwards to the sky, and his gun lay beside him.

Even in the moonlight, Heinrich could see the whiteness of his face.

The elder man bent down, and, unscrewing his flask, forced some brandy down the other's throat.

He felt the pulse. It was still beating and steady. Evidently the damage, if damage there had been, was slight.

He chafed the wounded man's hands, and going to the pool nearby, brought back some water in his hat, with which he bathed August's face and head.

At last he had the satisfaction of seeing the eyelids flutter and open, and recognition come into the eyes.

"August. . . ."

"Oh, Heini. What . . . Why . . .?"

"Yes, yes, August! Don't worry, my dear boy! What did he do to you?"

August struggled to a sitting position, clasping a hand to his throbbing head. Then he nodded into remembrance.

"Oh yes . . . I recollect everything now. . . ."

"Did he hurt you, August?"

"Not very much . . . Is he captured?"

"Yes: under lock and key. My word! he was a handful!"

It appeared that after Heinrich had departed to warn the town of the Monster's reappearance, August had waited until the Monster should present a fair target. He was still standing over the body of the fainting girl, and in that uncertain light it had not seemed wise, August explained, to fire, with so much risk of hitting the girl.

"No . . ." said Heinrich.

"And so I waited. And then, at last, he moved over to the right: quite clear of the girl. I decided to take a shot at him. I raised my gun, took aim as careful as the light would permit—and fired."

"And. . . .?"

"Well, whether or not I hit him again, I don't know."

"His hand was all covered with blood when we captured him. . . ."

"Yes, but that may have been from the first time I hit him. Anyway, I let him have one barrel, and he stopped dead in his tracks. I wondered for a second if I needed to fire again: he seemed so still. I expected him at any moment to topple over.

"Then he did a surprising thing. Without a sign of warning; without one preliminary sound; he suddenly leapt at me. That's the only word for it: just leapt at me. I hadn't expected it, it was the last thing in the world that I expected. I was taken completely off my guard.

"Clumsily I raised my gun to my shoulder, but I was very nervous. I missed the trigger and fumbled for it.

"At last I fired—just as the Monster knocked my gun aside. I remember hearing the report: and then, a most terrible concussion."

He fingered a swollen face with gentle touch.

"I think the gun must have slipped from my shoulder and, in recoiling, hit me on the temple. At any rate, I remember no more. . . ."

"Thank God he did no more than that," said Heinrich, piously.

After that, when August had recovered sufficiently to walk (albeit with an aching head) the two had set off for the town. But in that darkness it was easy enough to miss one's bearings, and after an hour's walking, each had come to the conclusion that they had lost their way.

It was just when they had decided to lie down at the foot of a tree, and await the day, that they caught sight of a faint glimmer of light.

They followed it, and came at last to the Hermit's hut.

"You knock, August. There's obviously somebody in."

August knocked, and a voice said:

"Come in."

The young man opened the door. The music did not cease: only softened a little, as the Hermit said:

"Come in, friends. Rest awhile."

Heinrich said:

"Can you tell us how to get out of this wood? We've lost our way."

"Well . . . I can try . . .!"

The two men stepped into the room, not unthankful for the prospect of a few hours' rest. Heinrich unloosed his rucksack, and threw it down on the floor by the doorway.

He cast an eye around the barely-furnished room. Then:

"Good God! August! Look!"

"Heavenly God! It's the Monster."

They were too amazed to speculate how it was, that the Monster, whom Heinrich had seen safely bound to a tree turn, could be sitting, apparently asleep in this remote cottage.

August, with a nervous clumsiness, raised his gun to be ready; at the same time setting the hammer to full-cock.

Heinrich whispered.

"Mind the old man, August, for God's sake!"

But now, that animal sense which always seemed so strong in the Monster, had warned him of danger. His eyes snapped open, and he was instantly on the alert.

Slowly, with an almost painful deliberation, he hoisted himself out of the chair in which he was sitting. His great staring eyes were narrowed down to tiny slits which missed nothing: and in them, the dark pupils burnt with an intensity of hate.

"Careful," said Heinrich, sensing danger.

The two men stood there, completely undecided: and (if truth be told) rather unnerved by this close contact with one whom they half-believed to be either something more, or something less, than human.

The Hermit too had realized that all was not well. He ceased playing: and the music came to a stop just as the Monster growled.

August's heart was beating almost to suffocation. He was not a coward, and many times he had faced death in the mountains from wild beasts and treacherous ravines. But here was something that was outside his ken: that added to natural danger the unknown element of supernatural horror.

Already this gaunt Monster, with his white face and furious eyes, had received the full discharge of his gun on two separate occasions: and his pride in his own undoubted marksmanship only filled August with apprehension the more.

He was, let us admit, undecided. And as he debated within himself the best course of action to take, the Monster decided for him!

There was a sudden spring: the great figure lunged, and caught the gun with a deftness astonishing in so clumsy-looking a creature.

August, taken completely by surprise, released his hold on the gun, and staggered back against the table, cannoning awkwardly into it.

There was a crash as the table went over.

The Hermit by now had risen to his feet: on his simple, calm face was an expression, not of fear, but of bewilderment.

He said sternly.

"What are you doing? This is my friend!"

"Friend!" Heinrich gasped, staring astonished at the spectacle of the kindly old man, placing his hand in a gesture of affection on the Monster's shoulder.

"Friend! Say 'fiend' rather!"

"Sir! I beg of you. . . ."

August shook his head pityingly. His gun was lying where the Monster had let it fall; but he saw that, for the moment, it was out of reach.

Heinrich said:

"Yes, 'fiend' is the word! This is the fiend that's been murdering half the countryside. Good heavens, man! Can't you see?"

The old man, with a wistful smile, shook his head; and August murmured gently:

"You pardon, sir. It is a sad affliction to be blind. . . ."

Heinrich said passionately:

"Why, sir, he isn't human! Frankenstein—the young Baron Henry—made him from the bodies of the dead!"

The Hermit shook his head. There was no alarm depicted on his face; only, as before, the pathetic bewilderment of a child among people who are talking of things he cannot understand. He looked . . . *lost*.

He turned to the Monster, his hand still on the other's shoulder.

"What are they saying?"

The Monster shook his head, growling. But tears rolled down his cheeks, as he saw the patient blind face raised to his, in a question that would never be answered.

He had half-turned from the two men as the Hermit spoke to him: and his attention was momentarily diverted from his enemies.

August, his watchful eyes on the gun, thought he saw his opportunity.

Holding his breath, the pulses drumming in his ears, he poised himself in readiness.

The Monster was searching the Hermit's face: he had, by now, turned almost completely away from the men.

Murmuring a silent prayer, August stepped swiftly across the room to where the gun was lying. He did not hesitate: he knew that this opportunity might never come again.

He bent down: his fingers closed on the cold walnut of the stock.

Then, suddenly, something hit him from above. The gun fell from his fingers as a great foot stamped on it, and the sweep of an enormous hand sent him reeling across the room, to crash through a pile of straw and wood against the edge of the fireplace.

It was Heinrich who first saw the danger. As August picked himself up (the Monster making no move either to follow or to shoot) his companion saw that the straw which had been scattered by August's headlong flight, had fallen into the open fireplace: and that already the flames were darting along the dry, inflammable material.

With a cry, Heinrich pulled August out of the way, just as the whole pile of straw went up in one huge tongue of flame. The hungry flames licked around the wooden beams of the fireplace, which were as dry as matchwood: they caught the wooden box in which the straw had been stored, and set fire to a little rush chair which stood by the open hearth.

For one moment, Heinrich, August and the Monster stood gazing, in paralysed horror, at this catastrophe which threatened them.

For one moment only they stood. Then, with a roar, the Monster flung himself across the room: not, indeed, at the two men who shrank back from his wild rush, but at the fire.

Growling and shouting, he stamped on the flaming straw, endeavouring to put it back into the fireplace, there to burn itself out harmlessly. With his great hands he beat at the charred and glowing wood of the mantelpiece, screaming with pain as his flesh came into contact with the scorched timber.

August, in the meanwhile, had seen his chance.

Taking advantage of the Monster's preoccupation with the fire, he darted across the room and seized the Hermit's arm.

"Quickly, now!"

Heinrich took the other arm, and between them they half-led the old man through the door. They were almost blinded by the smoke, and behind them, a sharper crackling told them that the roof had caught.

"Run!" August panted. "*He'll* be out in a minute!"

"Oh, my friend! the Hermit moaned. "Why have you done this?"

"Father," gasped Heinrich, "you must come with us. We have saved you from a certain death. We must come quickly away. . . ."

Supporting the blind man between them, they turned into a glade, and ran, stumbling and tripping through the still dark wood.

CHAPTER XVIII

THE NET WIDENS

STILL, it was not written that the Monster should die in that fire. His little drama was not yet played out; and that grim sequence which had commenced with the idle fancies of a student, had its course to run: had indeed, other lines to be spoken, and a grand finale to be faced.

Set upon a wider stage: rounding off the drama in the best traditional manner.

So that while the flames rose ever higher, scorching the Monster, and blinding him with smoke, he did not fall a victim to those flames.

Choking, blinded, half-fainting, he realized that the fire was greater than he: something told him that to stay was to die: and some subconscious instinct drove him to seek safety in flight.

Arms outstretched, he sought for the door. Furniture impeded him, tripping him up, and bruising his legs.

But at last his searching fingers found the door: the air blew fresher on his scorched face, cooling his smarting eyes and throat. He turned but once, to see the cottage wrapped in flames from lintel to roof.

Then he stumbled into the encircling wood, and guided only by instinct, made his way to the open country beyond.

Yet as though that instinct had in it some deeper purpose, than a mere flight from danger; his footsteps, unknown to him, were leading him towards one of the principal actors in this strange drama. The wheel was coming full circle.

Now, as the Monster made his uncertain way through the sombre aisles of the forest, he had no premonition that it was to the end of adventure that his feet were taking him.

And the end was not immediately upon him. Much had to be done, many lines to be spoken, before the players took their last bow, and the curtain fell upon the last act. . . .

"Out, out are the lights, out all;
And over each quivering form,
The curtain, a funeral pall,
Comes down with the rush of a storm. . . ."

Before that, the unravelled threads had to be gathered together to make the pattern complete, and a finish put to that wild story which had begun in a University laboratory more than ten years before.

So he stumbled on his journey, burnt, tortured, almost dropping from the pain of his wounds, and the exhaustion consequent upon the loss of blood.

He was a stranger to the wood: each new path was like its predecessor, and all seemed endless.

The branches tore at his face: his feet tripped over the exposed roots of trees. For four hours he wandered with ever increasing impatience, in this woody labyrinth, without once obtaining even a glimpse of the open country beyond.

But at last there seemed to his bewildered eyes a space at the end of a long avenue of trees; a score of glades had deceived him, and mocked his hopeful steps.

Once again his tired feet led him towards the gap in the trees, and this time, there was no mistake.

He broke through the trees into a meadow bright with gentian and buttercup, more brilliant than ever in the sunlight of early morning.

The world as yet was locked in slumber: only a few peasants were at work in the fields below, but coming across the meadow were a group of little children, evidently sons and daughters of the peasants. They were laughing and talking in the carefree way, stopping every now and then to gather flowers, or to roll in the grass.

They did not see the Monster approach: a little girl observed him, only as he was upon them; she screamed:

"The Monster!"

One shriek, and the children scattered before him, like chaff before the wind.

Yet they were not so quick that they escaped his swinging blows. There were cries of pain: a moment's astonished looking-back, at where the gaunt shape was continuing on its stumbling way.

Then with one accord, white-faced and trembling, they tore howling down the hill to the fields below.

In a few minutes a party had been organized. The cry "Monster!" shouted from the strong lungs of peasants, brought men and women hurrying across the fields.

They had heard, of course, of the Monster's escape from prison. They had heard, too, that he had been burnt to death in the blazing cottage.

"You say you've seen him, Christina?" a woman asked incredulously.

"Yes, Frau Schmidt."

"No lies, now. . . !"

"Ah come, Frau Schmidt," and elderly peasant expostulated. "Can't you see the child is nearly out of her wits with fright?"

The little girl, Christina, began to cry; and the woman, conscious of an unpopular move, added hastily:

"Oh, I didn't mean *that*. But you know," with a false, uneasy smile, "how children will have their little jokes. There, there, Christina dear. Don't cry! Daddy will go and kill the Monster now. . . ."

"Humph!" sniffed a young ploughman, "*that's* easier said than done. It looks as though nothing but the sacred bullet will kill him. Fire don't seem to mean a thing to him!"

"Ah, Fritz, you're right!" a greybeard added.

"Well, men," said the foreman, the father of the girl Christina, "let's be going. Which was did he go, Christina?"

The child shook her head, sniffing, dumb from horror. She pointed vaguely to the north-west, and the young ploughman nodded.

"That's in the direction of the cemetery. I always knew he was a vampire. Probably he's got a grave up there, where he rests."

The party of a dozen men set off for the cemetery. There was only one firearm among them, an ancient blunderbuss which was used for scaring the rooks and sparrows. But the others bore scythes and billhooks, and they all considered that their little gang, was a match for anyone: Monster or no Monster.

I will not describe their search in detail. Let it suffice when I say that they never found him.

He had gone, as the young ploughman with a rare accuracy had surmised, to the cemetery; and they passed within a few yards of where he was crouching behind some stunted yew-bushes.

Yet when they had spoken so glibly of finding the Monster, they had reckoned without their task. The cemetery was large, being indeed the principal cemetery of that district. And how extensive it was, they had never realized, until they were confronted with row upon row of tombstones, and vaultheads, and mausoleums.

They were hindered, too, by the fact that they had unconsciously accepted the young ploughman's dictum that it was *in* a grave that they would find him.

"Have we got to look in every grave?" said the greybeard, echoing the thoughts of them all.

The ploughman scratched his yellow, close-cropped head.

"Let's look around a bit," he said, unwilling to admit defeat so easily.

There was a perfunctory scanning of the serried rows of funeral monuments; the men showing a decided disinclination to venture far from the other' company.

At last:

"We'll never find him *here*," said the young ploughman, to the great relief of everybody.

Parson last Sunday had chilled their blood with "the Terror that walketh by noonday."

It seemed that they had met it several hours too soon.

"We'd better go and tell the Burgomaster," said greybeard; and sticking closely together, they went back the way they had come.

CHAPTER XIX

THE MONSTER COMES HOME, AND FINDS SOME FRIENDS

IT was not until the men had been gone for some time that the Monster arose cautiously from behind the bushes, and with a wary look around him, moved off in the direction of that part of the cemetery which contained the larger vaults and mausoleums.

He stumbled across graves newly-turned, and graves rank with the weeds of a century's growth. His clumsy feet smashed through the glass 'immortelles' crushing the waxen lilies and passion-flowers within.

His rough, torn hands snatched at the green tin vases on the tops of tombs, spilling the stale, brown water, and scattering their withered blooms in a wild, animal fury that owed much of its strength to the persistency with which his pursuers had hunted him.

At the end of a long avenue of graves he came suddenly upon a tall figure: a statue before which he halted in nervous suspicion. It was the figure of a Man, hanging by his hands from a wooden frame: a shape upon whose brow a coronet of spines had been set; and upon whose body were such disfiguring marks as marred the Monster's own.

On those pierced hands was blood: on those nailed feet: on that thorn-crowned head. And from a wound in the Man's side, blood had poured abundantly forth.

Blood. . . ! The Monster raised his hands and gazed at them. And as he gazed, so his memory harked back to the night before, when he had found that little white girl by the waterfall: had smoothed her soft cheeks, and held her limp tender body in his arms.

Back to his mind came the strange, exquisite pleasure of that moment: a pleasure as wonderful as it was impossible to analysis. He only knew that, as he held that tiny body in his arms; nay, more, with the very touch of his fingers against the downy softness of her cheek: a fire had seemed to run through every nerve and sinew of his body. But a fire which burnt only . . . and did not consume.

111

And then the men had come: the men who had raised the long tubes they bore: the dangerous terrible tubes, which roared and burnt; and struck on with the strength of many men.

At the thought of those men who had hurt him; who had taken the little white body from him; his fury became ungovernable. He saw the blood on the figure before him; and his muddled brain found some dim connection between the wounds on the hanging man, and the aching wound on his forearm.

With the roar of a baited, baffled animal, he suddenly rushed at the figure before him. He hung on the outstretched arms, and kicked at the overlapping feet.

With a shower of dust the figure tore loose from the nails that had supported it; and the Monster fell to the ground, clasping to his arms and painted body of the Nazarene.

He flung it aside, and rushed once again at the tall cross.

It was stuck deep into the stone base, and with the passing years, the wedges that had been driven in to support it, had almost fused with the mother shaft. Under the tremendous impact of his frenzied attack, the cross shifted a little, the strained wood creaking a protest; but did not fall.

Its strength only infuriated the Monster more. He drew back a dozen paces, and charged. Body and cross met with a shock that nearly tore his shoulder from its socket.

But his strength triumphed. There was a rending moan as the whole stone base of the Christus toppled backwards, and with a splintering of timber the cross crashed to the ground.

The Monster stood gazing down at the damage he had wrought, nursing his bruised shoulder; but, for all that, perfectly content.

"Good . . ." he mumbled, remembering the Hermit's lesson. "Good . . . good. . . ."

And now a curious thing had happened, which had the young ploughman been there to see, would have confirmed his worst fears.

The Monster was just about to move off on his aimless journey, when a last glance at the uprooted cross showed him an empty space yawning where the statue had once been.

It was, in fact, the entrance to a vault; whether the builders of the vault had used a fanciful means to hide the vault's entrance, or the Christus had been erected at some later date, long after the existence of the vault had been forgotten, it is impossible to say.

The Monster, at any rate, did not concern himself with these unprofitable speculations. Here, to his simple brain, showed a way of escape. With the instinct of a hunted animal, he waited no longer in decision than to assure himself, with a rapid glance into the hole, that a flight of steps, green with mold, but apparently sound, led downwards.

With a hasty glance around the cemetery, a glance that showed him no sign of any living thing, the Monster crept into the vault, and went gingerly down the steps.

He went gingerly, for it was in his nature to be cautious.

In his short life he had known no other than glances of horror, anger, disgust. The hand of a man had made him, and against him had the hand of every man been raised.

But it was of *men* that he went in fear: of no such hobgoblins as infected the imagination of the young ploughman and his friends.

Indeed, as he descended into the cool, dark vault, and the daylight died about him; as he came into the musty, airless gloom of the charnel-house and the damp, tired odour of things long hidden from the sun; it was as though he was coming home. Something of the same joy; that same strange, exquisite happiness that had possessed him, as he held the shepherdess in his arms, filled him now. But it was muted: a softer enjoyment altogether. His pulses did not race, nor veins throb, as on that night by the waterfall: but only in his breast contentment dwelt, a little warm lump: and he was glad.

Head raised high, he sniffed the air as an animal sniffs the evening. High above, chinks in the flagstones, and old rusty gratings, let through stray wisps of daylight, which struggled uncertainly against the gloom. . . and failed to triumph. He was in a vast network of vaults: of catacombs, rather: the common property of the better class families, who lived in and about the town of Frankenstein.

They had been built centuries before, and popular rumour had it that it was not for such funeral purposes that they had been constructed, but as the meeting hall of the infamous *Wehmgericht*, or secret tribunals, which struck terror through the Germany of the Middle Ages.

And there had seemed to be something of reason in the popular belief. For no cemetery-vault was ever of the elaborate construction of this.

High groined roofs arched overhead: each carved capital was decorated with the fantastic arabesques of monkish fancy: ape and man: and man that was half ape, and ape that was something more than man.

Here and there, too, were grilles of twisted ironwork and doors of fretted metal, which divided up into smaller sections, the vat expanse of the vaults.

Most of these gates were ajar: and the Monster passed unimpeded on his way through the ever-darkening vista of the catacombs.

He was happy. As I said, he snuffed the air as an animal sniffs the evening: and he was glad.

Dark remembrances; snatches of something that existed before life began; ran through his tortured brain, and gave him, if not content, at least the simulacrum of peace.

So happy, indeed, after his fashion, was the Monster, that it was with the greatest surprise that he was suddenly stopped short by the sound of voices: for his mood was such that he might have walked the whole length of the tombs without bestowing a thought on the world outside.

But these sounds of speech were couched in such urgent tones, that they penetrated through to his subconscious mind; setting him instantly alert, and banishing, in one second, that half-dreaming state in which he wandered through the tortuous ways of the place of death.

He stopped, shuffling hastily behind the shelter of a fluted pillar, listening.

A voice said:

"Br-r-r! I can smell the ghosts already. . . !"

"Ghosts?" the Monster whispered, "Ghosts. . .?"

He peered around the pillar.

In front stretched a dark expanse: gloom lighted vaguely with the straggling beams of daylight which filtered through the tiny apertures high above. There was a vista of tombs, and iron grilles, and floriated pillars.

That . . . and dim figures moving silently in the dimmer light.

A voice said:

"Which coffin do you want, Doctor?"

And a voice answered:

"Fool! You know the one I want . . . Find it: and quickly. . . ."

The Monster craned his neck around the pillar, eager to obtain a glimpse of the men who had anticipated his visit to the place that he had come, in such a short time, to regard as his home.

He strained his neck, seeking to catch a view of these interlopers.

Quietly, he waited; and presently, into the range of his vision came three men. One was tall, lean-faced, dressed after the manner of a man of quality (albeit a shabby one): the others were obviously his servants; one a hunchback, the other a lean, miserable fellow, who might have been anybody's slave.

The master snapped: "Franz, you are keeping me waiting! Do you know which coffin I want?"

Then followed some words in a tone too low for the listening figure to hear.

The man, Franz, nodded his head, evidently in agreement. For, signing to his companion, he hurried off behind some tombs, and out of the Monster's sight.

Minutes passed before they returned. But when, at last, they did come back, it was at a pace slower than that at which they had set forth.

Between them, the two men bore a coffin: and judging from the tardy pace at which they moved, a coffin that bore its full complement of human flesh.

"Put it up here," said their master, indicating the top of the tall sarcophagus against which he leaned.

"Bit of a weight, Doctor!" the hunchback grumbled.

"Never mind that!" the man addressed as "Doctor" snapped. "I want it up here. I can examine it better so."

With much grunting and straining, the two men hoisted the coffin on to the stone slab.

"All right," said the Doctor, "open it."

Franz approached with a chisel, which he thrust under the lid. He was about to force the wood when the Doctor suddenly laid a hand upon his arm.

"Stop! Franz; before you open it—read the name."

The dwarf rubbed his gnarled hand across the coffin's brass plate, wiping off the thick dust, and peering down at the faded letters.

"Well . . . read it."

"Died seventeen ninety-nine. Madeleine Ernestine, beloved daughter of . . ."

"Skip that," said the Doctor. "How old was she?"

"Aged nineteen years and three months. . . ."

The Doctor rubbed his hands, grinning his satisfaction.

"That's the one! Now, men, get to work!"

Two chisels, which shone in the light of the oil lamps, were thrust under the coffin lid. The dwarf exerted his strength; and from his hiding place the Monster watching the scene with intense curiosity, heard the wood creak and splinter.

"Good! It's giving . . . Now again. . . ."

The chisels were thrust deeper into the crack they had made. The dwarf and his companion put their whole weight on the steel levers, and with a final splintering smash, the lid came away, and fell heavily to the ground.

The two assistants backed away as the contents lay revealed; but the Doctor approached, with a frantic eagerness, to peer gloating into the coffin.

He turned to the two men, in sudden concern.

"Are you certain that you closed the vault door behind you?"

Franz nodded emphatically, but in the eyes of Ernst, his companion, the Doctor seemed to detect a certain doubt.

"Are you *positive?*" he repeated.

"Yes, Herr Doktor, positive."

He made a sign as of slitting his throat, and the Doctor smiled.

"Oh, *that* will happen to you anyhow," he said sarcastically.

He turned from the comtemplation of the corpse and slipped off briskly down a passage.

"Come along, men. We'll go and make certain that everything's all right. I shouldn't like to be caught here."

"Neither should I, the man Ernst grumbled.

The Doctor peered at him down his long nose.

"You're being paid handsomely for all you're doing. Now come along: and don't make to much noise."

They had hardly turned the corner, when the Monster shuffled out of his hiding-place.

Every sense was alert as he made his clumsy way over to the stone sarcophagus on which the coffin lay. His heart was beating to suffocation as he crept near to the open shell. Again that old emotion was upon him: he recognised that warm joy which had possessed him once before, as the little shepherdess lay in his arms

But now there was something more. Here, a stirring of the spirit was added to that first fierce stirring of the flesh. Here was a promised joy in surroundings that were full of an old familiar comfort, far away from the world of men; from that cruel world of pursuing feet and flaming tubes, and the mournful ululation of dogs.

Madeleine Ernestine was lying as sorrowing eyes had gazed on her for the last time, before the mutes had nailed down the oaken plank above her. The bandages were neatly tied around her small head, and on her maiden bosom the rosary was still entwined among the long slender fingers of her folded hands.

Even after these years, the delicate lawn of her shift was white, and the wreath of *immortelles* around her neck shone in the lamplight like stars.

But, these things apart, change, that rules us all, had not spared her. Her eyes had been closed by gentle fingers as she fell into the last sleep of all: yet those lids no longer curved over sapphire orbs.

The had sunk into the pits beneath: eyeballs were long collapsed and desiccated. And no roses bloomed now on those white cheeks: not even the roses of death.

There was, indeed, but one cheek remaining, and that seemed of black leather. The other had long since fallen in, to reveal the shining jawbone, and the little, even teeth.

And that pillar on which her small shapely head had once sat so proudly! Well, that was a pillar still; but its marble was pitted and corroded by time and time's grim assistant, the conqueror worm.

"Flesh fade and mortal trash, fall to the residuary worm. . . ."

Of all those glories which had once turned heads and fired young eyes in the street and Market Place, but one remained. Still from beneath the nunlike coif of her bandages, the golden hair peeped and struggled forth.

One brilliant strand, metallically lustrous in the lemon light, had escaped from the confining linen, and lay like a beam of tired sunlight across her face, following with a pathetic fidelity the changes that time had wrought in the once lovely features it caressed.

For it dipped into the empty sockets where once had lain her clear and sparkling eyes: it passed across those two flat slits which were all that was left of that small straight nose, "tip-tilted, like the petal of a flower" : and one curving ringlet lay across her mouth, as though to hide in mercy that lipless grin with which she mocked eternity.

But a clumsy hand rested in an odd gentleness of that drum-tight brow: bloodstained, blackened fingers caught up the golden strands of her hair.

And above her, the blue lips parted in a smile of tremulous joy.

"Good. . . ." said the Monster, stroking the bandaged head in affectionate gentleness. "Good . . . good. . . ."

Then from the passage came the sounds of footsteps and voices.

Silently the Monster shambled off, back to his hiding-place behind the pillar.

He saw the Doctor and the two men come up to the coffin: the Doctor with springy step and smiling face, his assistants with dragging feet and sullen mien.

"Well," said the Doctor, rubbing his hands, "I had to see for myself. But now that we know we're safe, we'd better start. That's the one," he said, pointing to the coffin. "Get to work!"

But Franz and Ernst stood still, exchanging suspicious, frightened glances.

The Doctor asked impatiently:

"What are you waiting for?"

Ernst crossed himself.

"Mercy on us!" he muttered.

The Doctor stamped his foot.

"Fools! Do you want me to send you to the gallows where you belong?"

"I'd be no worse than this," said Franz, defiantly.

The Doctor smiled icily, as he fixed the hunchback with his piercing glance.

"I wonder!" he said significantly. He added, "Are you ready?"

"Yes," they both mumbled.

"Very well, then. . . ."

From behind the pillar, the Monster saw the men lift the body and lay it on the ground.

"Carefully, now," the Doctor warned, as they laid it down.

"Pretty little thing, isn't she?" Franz asked, with grim humour.

"She *was*," the Doctor answered, unsmilingly, and added, "and will be again, if all goes well."

He bent gloating over the recumbent figure, prodding the corpse with his long forefinger.

"Seems solid enough. I hope her bones are firm."

Over his head Franz and Ernst exchanged glances. Franz shrugged his shoulders, and Ernst , putting a finger to his forehead, tapped with it in a significant gesture.

Franz picked up the chisels and hammer, and wrapped them in a piece of sacking.

"What about the coffin?" he asked sullenly.

"Oh, yes! You'd better put it back where you found it. Then no body need ever know that there have been visitors here."

Franz put his tools inside and, replacing the lid, the two men lifted the coffin from off the sarcophagus.

"It heaves lighter now," said Ernst.

"Yes."

"Well, Doctor, I guess that's all for to-night?" Franz asked: "May we go now?"

"Yes," the Doctor said, "you may. I think," he grinned, "that I shall stay here for a bit . . . I rather like this place."

The two men picked up the coffin.

"Now, Franz, don't forget about the Baroness! Most important. . . ."

"No Herr Doktor."

"And be careful that no one sees you leave."

"All right—all right!" said Ernst impatiently.

"And leave that lantern there for me. . . ."

"All right," said Ernst insolently.

The Doctor raised his eyebrows.

"Really!" he said. "Do I seem to detect a certain rebelliousness in the worthy Ernst, for whose sake I defrauded the executioner at Nüremberg of his fee?"

His tone was light, but his eyes, cold and piercing as steel.

Ernst turned to Franz with a shrug.

"Come on! Let's get away from this. And if there's much more like this; what do you say, friend; we give ourselves up and let 'em hang us?"

Franz answered:

"I would be better than this."

"You're right," Ernst nodded, "this is no life for murderers."

The Doctor laughed as the two men marched off down the passage.

"Oh, most magnanimous mice!" he chuckled.

He picked up a bundle which had been lying on the steps of the sarcophagus, and the Monster, watching the scene with uncomprehending eyes, saw him unwrap the napkin; to reveal a paper parcel of sandwiches, a loaf, some cheese and butter, a roast chicken, an apple, and a bottle of wine and a tin cup.

The comestibles the smiling Doctor placed on the top of the sarcophagus, using napkin as table cloth, and bringing from an inner pocket a little folding combination knife and fork, which utensils he wiped meticulously on the edge of his napkin.

He uncorked the bottle, and poured himself some wine.

"I give you;" he raised his cup: "the Monster!"

He picked up a sandwich, and commenced to eat it; staring around him with an air of great satisfaction.

"Snug little spot, you know," he murmured. "Could be made quite comfortable. Out of the way. Very unlikely to be disturbed."

The Monster, gazing out at all this play, grew more and more mystified, as each strange sequence followed its predecessor. Why had the man taken the lovely, desirable thing out of the box, only to leave her lying on the ground? And why did the man remain behind, when his two companions had gone?

And he was eating . . . that was good, to eat . . . and to drink . . .ah, that was good, too. . . .

A cautious and comprehensive glance had assured the Monster that the man did not possess one of the flame-throwing tubes. The lamp he did not connect with fire.

And because the sight of the man's eating reminded him that it was many hours since he himself had tasted food, he came forth from behind the pillar, mumbling uncouth sounds, which were the nearest to speech he could encompass.

The Doctor was raising the mug to his mouth when he heard those sounds.

He did not spill the wine, nor did he turn quickly around; nor run headlong for safety.

He did none of these things.

He put his cup deliberately and carefully down, turned slowly around, and surveyed the Monster with raised eyebrows.

"Oh!" said the Doctor. "I thought I was alone . . . Good evening!"

The Monster halted, blinking uncertainly, pointing a finger at him.

"Friend?" he asked.

Dr. Pretorius smiled.

"Yes, indeed, I hope so," he answered lightly. "Have a cigar. They're my only weakness."

The Monster ignored the offer, but his greedy eyes were fastened on the cold callation spread out on the stone tomb.

"Hungry? Help yourself."

The Monster advanced cautiously to the meat, as if he could hardly believe his vision. But nothing restrained him; and suddenly, with the speed of a darting hawk, his hand shot out and grabbed the chicken.

He watched the Doctor with suspicious, unwinking gaze, as his powerful hands tore the carcass apart, and thrust it into his jaws with a ravenous haste that made the Doctor smile.

But it soon became apparent to the Monster that Dr. Pretorius meant him no harm; and, as in all simple natures, his emotions were as evanescent as they were spontaneous and intense.

His suspicion departed after the third gulping mouthful, and he grinned his approbation of the chicken's quality.

"Food . . . good!"

"You like it?" the Doctor enquired with courteous grace. "Excellent! Have some more."

The Monster pointed a greasy finger at the wicker-bound carafe of wine.

"Wine?" the Doctor asked, picking up the bottle.

The Monster shook with eagerness. He said (though his mouth was full):

"Drink . . . good!"

"Not always," murmured the Doctor, "but I think metaphysics are hardly you *métier*. . . ."

He poured out a cupful of the wine, and the Monster mumbled:

"Mmmm! *Drink* . . . good . . . good. . . !"

Pretorius handed him the cup, observing with a thoughtful grown, his growing friendship.

"There . . . I hope you like it."

Dropping the chicken-bone without another thought, the Monster clutched at the proffered cup with both eager hands. He lifted it to his mouth and drank greedily and noisily: not putting the cup down, indeed, until he banged it empty on the cold stone.

"Good . . ." he said, smacking his lips.

"Have some more," said the Doctor, pointing to the food.

The Monster picked up the apple and ate it with every sign of enjoyment.

"You make man like me?" he asked, munching away.

"No," said the Doctor, measuring his words, "woman . . . friend to you. . . ."

He glanced downward as he said it, and the Monster's eyes followed the direction of his glance.

"Woman?" He seemed uncertain. "Friend!" He knew that word. "*Friend!* I want friend . . . like me."

The Doctor was very thoughtful now.

He said, though it was more to himself than to the Monster:

"I think you can be most useful, And, if necessary you will add a little force to the argument."

He picked up the bottle and drank a little.

He asked idly, lighting a cigar:

"Do you know who Henry Frankenstein is, and who *you* are?"

The gaunt face was set with purpose. The Monster seemed to be recollecting . . . and it was with a struggle.

At last he said slowly:

"Yes . . . I know. Made me . . . from dead."

He added, with a sort of gloating satisfaction that made the Doctor, in spite of his cynicism, uncomfortably depressed:

"I love dead . . . hate living."

"Good," said Pretorius, lightly, shaking off the momentary depression: "you are wise in your generation. We must have a long talk, and then I have an important call to make."

"Woman . . ." the Monster croaked, "friend. . . ."

He stared down at the tattered shreds of her who had once been so beautiful: and as though by some potent imaginative force, he could recreate her lost loveliness, he smiled, and murmured:

". . . Wife. . . ."

The Doctor was thoughtful, indeed, as he watched this curious play.

CHAPTER XX

THE TURN OF THE SCREW

IT was late that same night that Minnie knocked on the door of the library, and not-too-good-tempered voice bade her come in.

She said, fully conscious of the fact that she was the bearer of unwelcome news:

"That Doctor Pretorius is here again, sir."

Henry had been standing by the fireplace as she entered, examining some papers. With a gesture of annoyance, he put the papers down on a little table.

"There; I knew it! Send him away, Minnie! I *won't* see him!"

"I certainly will," said Minnie.

She opened the door . . . and Dr. Pretorius stood just without.

"Well!" she said, too astonished to protest.

"Your master is in, I take it?" he asked, with his falsest smile.

He pushed past her into the library, ignoring Henry's frown, and the coldness of his manner.

"Oh, Baron, there you are . . . I am sorry to trouble you like this . . . but, you see. . . ."

"I was just going out," said Henry curtly.

"Alone?"

"With my wife . . . as you see." He pointed to the doorway, and the Doctor turned to see Elizabeth standing there, already dressed for walking. Her manner was, if anything, even more frigid than her husband's.

But frowns were wasted on the urbane Doctor Pretorius.

He said, evenly:

"Baroness, I have not had the opportunity of offering my felicitations on your marriage. Pray accept them now."

"Dr. Pretorius," was the answer, delivered with a cold, grave dignity, that it was somehow impossible to mock, or brush aside, "I don't know what your business is with my husband; but whatever it may be, I tell you frankly that I am not frightened of it, or of you!"

"Henry," she added more warmly, "has been very ill. He is therefore in no state to be alarmed or annoyed. Your visit now, Doctor, is most unwelcome."

She turned from the angry Doctor with a shrug, and walked over to the fireplace.

"Henry, I heard the carriage drive up. I shall see that the baggage is put in. Then," she added, with a significant glance at the doctor, "we are leaving."

She picked up her muff, and moved towards the door. At the threshold she stopped to say:

"I shall expect you immediately. Doctor Pretorius, good-bye!"

It was with ill-concealed annoyance that the Doctor watched the Baroness walk across the hall, and pass through the open front door.

But his anger seemed to disappear as soon as she had gone: overwhelmed in a matter of much greater importance.

He turned to Henry with a quick pleading. He said earnestly:

"I think you know why I have come, Henry. . . ."

He paused, scanning eagerly the face before him for signs of relenting.

And, apparently, he saw something there which encouraged him to continue, for he went on:

"All the preliminary preparations are made: *my* part of the experiment is complete. I have," he said with an impressive deliberation, "completed a perfect human brain. . . ."

"A brain!" Henry echoed, his resentment forgotten in the wonder of the thing he heard.

"A brain, Baron," smiled the Doctor, very tactfully concealing his delight at the other's ready interest. "A perfect human brain: already living—but dormant."

He paused, before he added slowly:

Everything is now ready for you and me to begin in our supreme collaboration."

His piercing eyes seemed to bore into Henry's soul as he said it, and for several second the young man wavered in resolution.

But even as his imagination envisaged the wonderous potentialities of the Doctor's experiment, another thought came to stay his hand, to strengthen his resolve.

Again he saw the flames lick the rotten-dry wood of the ancient mill: again his eyes smarted, and his throat burnt, as he fought with the Monster: once more the ground rushed towards him with sickening speed, as he was thrown from the mill's top.

He covered his face with his hands: his body swaying with the agony of his spirit.

"No . . . Oh, no, no, no! . . Don't tell me of it! I don't want to hear!"

He suddenly dropped his hands, and faced the anger of the thwarted doctor.

"Do you hear? I've changed my mind. I . . . won't . . . do . . . it!"

Pretorius, in anger almost uncontrolled, shouted: "I expected this!"

"Of course," said Henry insolently, with a shrug of his shoulders, "I have been quite plain with you. Then why are you so disappointed?"

The Doctor said quickly:

I thought we might need another assistant. Possibly *he* can persuade you."

He walked across the room as he said it, and shut the door, turning the key in the lock.

Henry said firmly:

"Nothing can persuade me!"

"No?" the Doctor asked, his eyebrows raised in bland impudence: "Well . . . we shall see."

He walked across the room once more: but this time to the tall french windows. Henry watched him in astonishment as he pull aside the heavy drapes, and flung wide the sashes of the window.

And then:

"No! For God's sake, Pretorius: not *that.*"

"Dear, dear," the Doctor lisped, smiling mockingly at Henry. "Yet, you know, he is quite harmless . . . except, of course, when crossed. . . ."

The Monster had stood just within the windows while the men had spoken. The Doctor signed to him: and he pulled the heavy drapes together.

Then he had turned, and looked long at the man whose mad genius had contrived his body from the flesh of the dead.

"Frankenstein . . ." the harsh voice croaked.

Henry's face was white, and his hands trembling as he looked from the Monster to Pretorius, and then from Pretorius to the Monster.

The Doctor, seeing his agitation, observed smoothly:

"Yes, Henry: there have been developments since he came to me. . . ."

The Monster did not seem to be paying any attention to the Doctor's remarks. His staring eyes never left the pale face of his creator: and on his own face was a look that Henry shuddered to see.

The creature, holding Henry's gaze in the unwinking regard of an alligator, raised both his hands, and waved them up and down.

"Sit . . . down. . . ."

"I should . . . if I were you, my dear Baron."

Henry sat down.

He asked breathlessly, running his tongue across his dry lips.

"What do you want?"

"You know," came the cold, unnatural tones.

Henry, in a sudden disgust, shouted at the Doctor:

"This is *your* work!"

Blandly: "Yes. . . ."

Henry, white with terror and rage, stormed at the Doctor:

"I'll have no hand in such a monstrous thing!"

"Rather a change of mood since the other night," sneered the other.

"I wasn't myself," Henry snapped. "I have had time since then to realize how foolish I'd be to go on with this."

"But, my dear Baron, it's too late now to draw back."

"*Why* is it?" Henry demanded excitedly. "I *won't* go on with it."

A cold voice, instinct with a menace all the more deadly, in that tones were so utterly flat and unemotional, said:

"Yes . . . must!"

"Pretorius," Henry shrieked, "get him out! I won't even discuss this, until he is gone!"

The Doctor turned to the Monster.

"Go now," he said, as though he were accustomed to be obeyed.

But something had happened to the usually tractable Monster. Without emotion, he shook his head.

"No!"

Pretorius said sternly:

"*Go!*"

The Monster turned and walked over to the french window. Then he stopped, and repeated:

"No!"

He walked back to Henry's chair, and stood for several seconds, towering menacingly above the shrinking man.

Slowly, and with difficulty, he said"

"Must . . .do . . . it."

Henry, writhing under the sense of impotence and humiliation, swayed on his seat as he gripped the chair with both hands.

"Pretorius," he moaned, "for God's sake take this *thing* away. Nothing can make me go on with this!"

A growl sounded above him; and a heavy fist was raised in a threatening gesture.

"Stop that," Pretorius commanded. "Here: come this way!"

He caught the growling Monster by the arm, and half-led, half-pulled him, to the french window. With his free hand, he pulled the drapes aside, and opening the window, thrust the Monster forth.

As he closed the glass doors, the Doctor reopened them for one second to snap:

"No! stop that growling."

He slammed the doors and readjusted the heavy curtains.

Henry was still sitting in the chair: white-faced and apparently exhausted. As the Doctor came towards him, he sighed:

"Thank God he's gone . . ." And as if in afterthought, "though where the poor creature can go, I've no idea."

"Oh, that's all right," said the Doctor evenly. He did not explain that outside the french windows, Franz had been waiting, to see that the monster would be available when required.

Nor indeed, did Henry know that at that moment, dwarf and Monster were hiding behind some privet bushes at the side of the main entrance.

Before the great doorway the carriage was waiting, the horses pawing the ground uneasily and champing at their bits.

Through another french window, the dwarf and his companion could see Elizabeth standing in the hall, while Minnie was walking across, laden with furs and wraps.

The butler entered, and through the open door Franz heard Elizabeth say:

"Put the bags in the carriage, and I'll be out in a moment. Go and tell the Master to hurry, Minnie, or we shall miss the stage."

Franz could see the hesitation in every line of the maid's face, as she said:

"Excuse me for being so nervous, my lady, but I don't like leaving you alone."

Elizabeth smiled gratefully at the woman's concern.

"Oh, nonsense! Run along: I'll be all right."

"I hope so, my lady."

The maid left the hall, and Franz's heart almost stopped from excitement. He had perceived already that, from where Elizabeth was standing, the front door was hidden behind a jutting corner of the room. The butler was superintending the loading of the bags: Minnie had gone to fetch the Baron: Elizabeth was quite alone.

With trembling fingers he pulled at the sashes of the window. He realized that there was not a minute to be lost.

It was obvious that only the latch across the windows was down, and that they had not been bolted to the floor.

They gave a little, and he slipped his strong fingers underneath.

Another pull: and the sashes parted.

He waited a long second, with racing heart, to see if she had heard the noise. Only a second; before he tiptoed across the hall to where the unsuspecting Elizabeth waited.

Then a cold draught warned her of danger. She turned, saw Franz's crouching body, and screamed.

Minnie, entering at that moment, saw Franz leap upon Elizabeth, and despite her frantic struggles, pick her up in his strong arms and carry her, kicking and screaming, to the open window.

And she saw, too, a face outlined against the darkness beyond the open window: a white, staring face that was only too hatefully, terrifyingly familiar.

There, white, with the cold, dead whiteness of a fish's belly, was the staring face of . . . the Monster!

CHAPTER XXI

THE DOCTOR SHEWS HIS HAND

IN the library Pretorius had just said:

"Oh course, my dear Baron, I should hate to coerce you in any way," when a woman's shrill scream shattered the night.

"Henry, Henry, Henry!"

"God, Doctor! It's Elizabeth."

He dashed to the door and flung it wide as the screams came to his ears with a new and dreadful intensity.

"Henry . . .Oh, Henry, Henry!"

He rushed out of the library, and headlong down the broad passage that led to the hall.

Minnie was standing there sobbing, and Henry caught her by the shoulders as he came up.

"Minnie, what has happened?"

"The Mistress . . ."

"Yes, yes, he begged: "tell me!"

The servants by this time had gathered around, their faces white with anxiety.

"Oh, sir, she's gone!"

"Where?" The word cracked like a whip.

"The Monster . . . he got her! I saw it!"

Henry's head sank on his breast. He muttered:

"I might have guessed it. This is Pretorius's doing."

Then with a sudden reviving decision, still holding the sobbing Minnie:

"Quick! Get search parties! There's not a moment to lose!"

He turned to the butler.

"You, Schleicher, are in charge. I leave the arrangements to you."

The butler, and old soldier, bowed stiffly.

"Very well, Highborn; I shall do my duty."

"Then go," said Henry: and the servants, under the command of Schleicher, were marching off in the direction of the door, when there came a sudden startling interruption.

There was a crash, as of china smashing.

Everyone halted, and turned in the direction from which the noise had come.

It *had* been the smashing of china; in fact, of a large and valuable Sèvres vase, which had stood on a small table in the hall. But now it was in fragments; and those fragments were scattered about the feet of Doctor Pretorius, who raised his eyes from an unemotional examination of the remains, to a piercing regard of the people before him.

He said slowly, with measured deliberation:

"Stop a moment! I charge you—as you value your mistress's life, to do nothing, and say nothing of this episode."

He looked at Henry, still supporting the distressed Minnie in his arms, and smiled cynically.

"I assure you, my dear Baron, that the Baroness will be safely returned—if you will leave everything to me."

In despair, Henry turned to the assembled servants, whose glowering looks showed what impression this speech had made on them.

"Schleicher, I cancel my orders. Nothing can be done."

"But, Highborn. . . ."

Henry shook his head, and the butler bowed in ill-concealed disgust.

"Very well, Baron."

When the servants had gone, Henry turned wearily to the Doctor.

"Let us go back to the library. . . ."

As they walked along the passage, he said bitterly:

"Well, for the time being—you have won."

Pretorius smiled as he held the library door open, and Henry passed through.

"And yet," he mused, as they sat down, "I wonder if you will think so badly of me, when you see how far I have progressed.

He leaned forward and laid a hand on the young man's knee, and his voice was almost tender as he continued:

"Henry, once upon a time you were my most promising pupil. Ten years ago I shouldn't have had to *plead* with you. . . ."

"Where is Elizabeth? Tell me that!"

The Doctor shrugged his shoulders, as one might at the petulance of a child. He murmured patiently:

"Safe . . . as I told you."

Henry said:

"I wonder if I can trust you . . . or *him*."

"Both . . . we are equally well trained!"

"You never liked the Baroness." Henry said sullenly.

"The dislike, I think, was mutual," was the airy answer. "Though, of course, she had less reason to justify *her* enmity."

"Oh," said Henry, with a cynical look at the shabby professor, "and what justification had yours?"

Quietly:

"That I dislike, and mistrust, petticoat influence."

Henry said:

"I understand. . . ."

"Good," said the Doctor smiling. "Our bargain then, is this: that you will help me to make the woman the Monster's mate. And, in return, I undertake to deliver the Baroness to you, safe and sound. . . ."

"And what else," Henry asked grimly, "is demanded of me?"

"Nothing at all. You are only required to do what *he* demands."

"Very well," said Henry, with an air of finality. "I have no choice. But," and here he caught the Doctor's arm in a grasp that made the old man wince, "if one hair of her head is injured, then God help you! For I'll kill you so slowly and so horribly, that you'll shriek for death . . . and I shall not listen to you."

He flung the white-faced Doctor from him, and turned towards the door.

"Are you ready, Doctor?

"Yes," Pretorius muttered, with a spiteful glance, rubbing his bruised arm.

"We will take my carriage. Where is your laboratory?"

"In the old watch tower on the heath. I rented it for a year. . . ."

"Very well. Let us go!"

CHAPTER XXII

"...IT MUST BE SOUND ... AND YOUNG..."

IT was a week later that Henry and the Doctor sat facing each other across the long laboratory table.

They were in the Doctor's workroom, high up in the old watch tower, where, for these past seven days, they had assembled, with infinite care, living organs in a synthetic human body; keeping each alive by an independent vascular system, until all were assembled in their marvelous interdependence, and they worked together in that unity of effort and purpose that we call "life."

It was a lonely place, this tower in which the Doctor had established his workshop. For years it had remained derelict; shunned by children because of its reputation as an abode of ghosts; and too far off the main roads to attract the attention of tramps and such like.

What money its present owner had expended on it, had been confined to purposes purely utilitarian. There had been no efforts to render the place anything more than merely habitable. Nothing done, indeed, to transform it into a home; although the Doctor had given up altogether his house in the town.

So that Henry had spent a most uncomfortable week, passing wretched, sleepless nights on a straw-filled pallet: finding only an occasional solace in his work; and tortured by the ever-recurring thoughts of Elizabeth.

He knew that the Doctor had meant every word of his threat: that if any efforts were made by the Baron's servants to find her, her husband would lose her altogether.

Franz, accordingly, had taken a note to Schleicher, positively forbidding any search: and Henry knew the man well enough to feel confident that his orders would be obeyed.

And there had been something else to disturb his peace of mind;

The Bride of Frankenstein

an annoyance that he had vainly asked the Doctor to prevent. That was the constant supervision of the Monster.

No matter how intricate the work upon which they were engaged; when a clumsy hand, upon a scale or measuring-glass, might well rob their great experiment of any chance of success; the door would suddenly be flung open, and the Monster would walk in. Time and time again, Henry had pleaded with the Doctor to forbid the Monster to come to the laboratory; and each time Dr. Pretorius had laughed maliciously.

"He's interested in his future wife, poor fellow! Weren't you Henry?" he asked, with a sly grin.

"How do you expect me to be able to concentrate on my work with that great . . . *zany* hanging over me?"

The Doctor would shrug his shoulders, murmuring that, really, Henry had much better endure it. After all, it would soon be over. So, for seven days, Henry had worked under these unpleasant conditions, spurred on by the hope of release, and the desire to see Elizabeth once more.

"Are you sure she's safe?" he had asked Pretorius on this night, as he had asked a hundred times before.

The Doctor raised his eyebrows as he looked up from examining a test-tube.

"The Baroness? Oh yes! to be sure. She is well, and will be safely returned . . . if you will proceed."

Henry sighed, and turned again to the contemplation of a heart that was beating under the stimulus of an electric motor.

Pretorius got up from his chair, and walked around the table.

He stood behind Henry's chair, looking over the young man's shoulder.

For several seconds he watched the heart-beats registering on the rate-counter: at the sensitive finger of the Baron, as he adjusted the various screws which controlled the strength of the current, and the saline solution in which the strangely living heart was immersed.

He smiled:

"It is interesting to think, Henry, that once upon a time, we should have been burned at the stake as wizards for this experiment."

Henry said quickly, peering into the glass tank where the heart lay:

"Doctor . . . I think the heart is beating . . . Look!"

"On its own?"

"Yes . . . Look at it. . . ."

The Professor leaned over his shoulder, peering into the tank with eyes that burnt in the fever of fanaticism.

"*It is!* Oh . . . if only. . . ."

Henry said:

"It is beating right enough . . . Only, the rhythm of the beat is uncertain."

"Increase the saline solution. Is there any life yet?"

Henry shook his head.

"No: not life itself yet. This is only the simulacrum when the electric force is applied."

Pretorius patted the young man's shoulder.

"Never mind," he said, "we must be patient. The human heart is more complex, remember, than any other part of the body."

The indicator was now showing a rapid acceleration in the beats. The spark gap at the top of the instrument was flashing with continuous, even, sparks; and now the movement of the aorta could be clearly distinguished.

"Look! the beat is increasing, Henry!"

"Yes."

In a breathless silence, the two men watched the indicator for several minutes.

Then:

"It has stopped!"

Pretorius enquired anxiously:

"Shall I increase the current?"

"No," said Henry, shaking his head in nervous exasperation, "this heart is useless. I must have another; and it must be sound . . . and young."

"Yes," said Pretorius thoughtfully, "sound and young . . . Let me see . . . Franz!"

"Herr Doktor?"

Pretorius looked very hard at the dwarf for a moment, before he spoke; and had Henry been watching, he might have thought he saw the Doctor *wink* at his assistant.

He said, slowly and deliberately:

"Franz, you must go to your friend at the Accident Hospital. . . ."

"What we need," Henry explained tersely, "is a victim of sudden death. A female: young, preferably. Can you do it?"

Franz peered at Henry from between narrowed lids as he said: "Herr Baron, you promised me a thousand crowns. . . ."

Dr. Pretorius waved his hand in a lordly gesture.

"It will be well worth it . . . and the Baron will pay."

"Yes, yes," said Henry impatiently. "Go and get it."

Franz unbuttoned the overall he wore when engaged in the laboratory.

"I'll try," he said, as he opened the door and went out.

"Well," said the Doctor, "we can only wait. I don't suppose he'll be long. . . ."

Henry murmured, not altogether at his ease:

"There are always accidental deaths occurring. . . ."

"Always," the Doctor answered airily: but in his mind there was a picture of Franz tramping across the heath, keeping a wary eye open for any young woman he might meet alone. He had not thought it necessary to tell Henry that the Accident Hospital had long since refused to supply him with cadavers.

But the heart, if he knew Franz, would certainly fulfil Henry's requirements . . . even to the sudden death. . . . With grim humour he smiled . . . and still smiling, he asked Henry if he wouldn't care to overhaul the preparations, while they were waiting for Franz to return?

Henry nodded, and rose from the table.

"First the diffuser . . ." he said.

The Doctor walked across the room, and pulled a lever set in the wall.

There was a sudden rumble of hidden machinery, and the ceiling divided into two leaves, which rolled back to reveal the starlit sky above. As the doors opened, two heads leant over the trap, and a voice shouted:

"Want us to start, Herr Doktor?"

Pretorius shook his head.

"No. I'm only giving the apparatus a final over-haul. For God's sake don't let go the kites until I order it. . . ."

"No, sir!"

"Stand aside, Henry. I'm going to test the diffuser."

Another lever this time: and a tall column of insulated porcelain globes shuddered, moved, and swung into the centre of the room directly above a table set on gleaming metal legs, such as surgeons employ for the operations.

"Henry, move the table a little. See, it's too near the edge of the platform."

Henry moved the table, and the Professor nodded.

"Stand aside!"

He pulled the lever further over: and now the glittering column of the diffuser started slowly to rise through the open trap-door, the table following directly beneath, moving upwards on cables attached to the four corners of the platform on which it rested.

Up, and up; beyond the framework on the roof: high above the heads of the roof-top watchers, until the operating table stood at the tower's very top, while above it, reaching into the sky, towered the strange shape of the diffuser.

"Perfect!" said the Professor, contentedly, turning the lever once more, and reversing the motion.

As the operating table's platform sank to rest on the laboratory floor, and the diffuser swung back in its cradle, to the farther wall, the door opened, and Franz came in.

He walked up to the table and tossed a bundle down on the table, where it fell with a dull, sodden sound.

"You owe me a thousand crowns, Baron.

Henry's feverish fingers unwrapped the heart from the bloodstained rags in which it was wrapped.

His own beat almost to suffocation, and his mouth was dry as he saw the fresh brightness of the blood: saw the evidence, in the ragged veins and torn sinews of unskilful surgery.

He shuddered as he picked it up, and with deft, practised fingers attached the artificial conduits to the ragged ends of the arteries.

He switched on the current, started the motor; and the warm blood began to pump into the organ.

A minute's anxious watching, then a triumphant cry.

"It's beating perfectly, just as in life. Oh, if only I could keep it going until. . . ."

Franz grinned.

"It was a very fresh one," he said.

A foot stamped on his with savage force, but the Doctor's face betrayed no emotion.

Henry looked up in a sudden alarm.

"Where did you get it, Franz?"

"I . . . gave the gendarme fifty crowns. . . ."

"What gendarme?" was the suspicious question.

"Well . . . it was a . . ."

Franz looked at the Doctor as he fumbled for an explanation, and behind Henry's back the Doctor framed the words "police case."

Sighing in relief, the man said:

"It was a police case, Herr Baron."

Henry sank back into his chair. If only he were free of all this horrible intrigue: if only Elizabeth and he. . . .

The Doctor was saying, in his lisping affected tones:

"Yes . . . very sad . . . but we can't bother about that now. Can I do anything?"

"No, no, no," Henry said, closing his eyes, and shaking his head. "I can work better alone."

Without a word, Pretorius signed to Franz to go out; and as the hunchback opened the door, the Doctor, with one last glance at Henry busy with the heart, followed his servant.

CHAPTER XXIII

". . . UNTIL TO-MORROW, BARON!"

IT was nine hours later that the door of the laboratory opened, and the Monster came in with scuffling tread.

His eyes gleamed as he saw that Henry, worn out with unceasing work, had fallen asleep at the table. The Doctor was standing in the room; but he had not awakened Henry, realizing the exhaustion that had overtaken him.

But the Monster was made of less discerning stuff. He shambled over to the table, and grasping the shoulders of the sleeping man, shook him roughly.

Henry awoke, blinking.

"Work!" said the Monster.

Henry, stupid from fatigue, murmured:

"Where's Elizabeth? Have you brought her?"

The gaunt head slowly shook, while a cunning gleam shone in the cold eyes.

"She wait . . . I wait . . . !"

Henry caught sight of Pretorius standing by the window.

"Doctor, I'm exhausted . . . I must get sleep!"

The inexorable voice by his side said:

"Work!" It added "Finish—then sleep!"

Henry shook his head, running his hands distractedly through his hair.

"I can't work like this," he moaned. "I *can't!* Pretorius, he must go away. Send him away, for God's sake!"

The Doctor seemed to meditate, as he observed the Monster: and Henry cried:

"For *your* sake, if not for mine, send him away! Doesn't your commonsense tell you that I can't work, with him constantly worrying and annoying me?"

The Doctor nodded.

"I'll settle him," he smiled grimly.

He turned to a little side-table on which were a bottle of whisky and some glasses. He picked up the bottle and a glass and walked over to where the Monster stood.

"Drink?" he asked, amiably.

"Mmm . . ." the Monster growled delightedly.

"Come over here, then," said the Doctor, leading him away from Henry. He poured out a generous measure of whisky, adding (though the Monster did not realize this) an equally generous sleeping draught.

Smiling, he handed the glass to the Monster, and eager hands grasped it.

"Drink . . . drink . . . *good*. . . ."

The Doctor nodded, watching the Monster intently as he drank. He saw the gaunt face light up with enjoyment: then, a second later, the face sobered, as the Monster staggered back, to fall across the sofa.

Pretorius waited until he was completely unconscious. He lifted the legs on to the sofa, and threw a blanket over the great body.

"Now—that'll settle you for a while!"

He turned to Henry, smiling.

"Well . . . now we can proceed: yes?"

Henry shook his head, staring at the Doctor with haunted eyes.

"Elizabeth . . . she's dead. . . ."

"No," the Doctor answered gravely, "she is alive and she is well. . ."

Henry leapt from his chair, and strode across to where the Doctor stood. His fists were clenched and his weak face working with rage, as he screamed:

"I don't believe it!"

The Doctor waved his hand.

"Pooh! Calm yourself, my boy! Would you like proof?"

"What proof, that I could believe?" Henry asked disdainfully.

The Doctor ignored the sneer, and said quietly:

"You want proof?"

"Oh," Henry pleaded, "give me *some* proof, Doctor, I am going mad, with the worry of wondering where she is . . . Please!"

The Doctor strode across to the cupboard, opened it, and lifted out a small box with wires attached, which Henry recognized as the voice-carrier the Doctor had one showed him.

He placed it on the table, and turned a switch set on the top of the instrument.

With a glance at the white-faced Henry, the Doctor said slowly, into the box:

"Baroness, are you there?"

A moment's pause, then in blurred, metallic tones:

"Yes. Who is that?"

The Doctor made a sign to Henry, and trembling with an agitation he could not repress, he walked over to the instrument.

"Speak," said the Doctor. "Speak, and she will answer."

The voice asked:

"Is that you, Henry?"

"Yes, yes. . . this is Henry!"

With tears of joy running down his cheeks the young man whispered:

"Are you quite safe, Elizabeth?"

"Henry—yes, I'm safe . . . how long? Come for me soon, dear. I am in a cave and . . ."

The line went dead, and Henry shouted:

"Elizabeth . . . Elizabeth. . . ."

"Be quiet! hissed the Doctor.

"But," said Henry in astonishment, "I was speaking to her, and . . ."

"Will you, Baron," said the Doctor, with an ominous quiet, "kindly proceed with your experiments."

Henry shrugged his shoulders and turned towards the laboratory table. As he did so he noticed that Franz had come in; that the dwarf was standing, with his back to the door, observing the Doctor with an oddly grim smile twisting his lips.

But the Doctor had seen him come in, yet too late to switch off the talking-machine. And the Doctor had seen too, the recognition dawn in the dwarf's bloodshot eyes, as the metallic voice came from the box.

And the Doctor had shuddered at the slow smile with which the dwarf had gazed into his eyes.

Henry said:

"Thank God she's alive, Doctor!"

"Yes," tersely, "you heard her. All is well. . . ."

"Yes; she's alive. . . !"

"As soon as our work in completed she will be returned to you."

He walked over to the table, and stood watching the pulse-counter.

"The heart is beating more regularly now."

"Yes," said Henry, "it has been beating for nine hours."

Silence: while the Doctor observed the regular flashing of the spark. He nodded.

"Not yet . . . but soon . . ." he murmured. "And the brain?"

"Perfect . . . and already in position."

"Then," said the Doctor, with a covert glance at Franz, "we are almost ready."

"Almost . . . said Henry, watching the indicator. "Almost . . . Doctor, shall we put the heart in now?"

"Yes. . . ."

"Franz!" Henry called, rising from his chair. "Help me to wheel the body over."

The two wheeled the table on which the body was lying, across to the laboratory table. Henry pulled back the sheet that covered the body, and removed the swabs with which the gaping wound in the chest had been temporarily filled.

Pretorius picked up the glass container in which the heart reposed.

"It's beating quite normally now."

"Bring it over. And bring the tongs."

Henry bent over the figure, freshening the edges of the incision with a scalpel so as to render their ligature the easier afterwards. He turned to Pretorius.

"Now. . . !"

The Doctor, with deft fingers, disconnected the artificial veins from the living heart; and picking it up in the tongs, dropped it neatly into the gaping pectoral cavity. The thing was done in a second.

Nor did Henry waste any time. With agile fingers he connected the veins of the heart and body, released the clips that had closed the ends of the arteries, massaged the heart for one minute to restore the action, and sutured the edges of the cavity with needle and thread.

Sighing heavily, he turned to the Doctor.

"Until to-morrow, she will have to live on an artificial blood supply. But to-morrow night, we'll try the great experiment. Let us see if perchance the very forces that set alight the spark of life in the primeval waters of our earth, can not yet fire that same spark in this body we have made: living, yet not alive. . . ."

CHAPTER XXIV

"THE STORM IS RISING. . .!"

TWENTY-FOUR hours later, the three men stood together in the laboratory room of the tower.

Through the open window, they could see the clouds scurrying across the full moon, driven by the fierce wind of the mounting storm.

Suddenly the sky was lit with a vivid flash of lightning, and from afar off came the low rumble of thunder.

Franz said:

"The storm is rising: listen!"

"And the barometer is still falling," the Doctor added. He turned to a gauge that hung on the wall, and examined it carefully.

"The force-recorder registers an exceptional figure. The air is heavy with electricity."

Henry nodded.

"It's going to be a terrific storm," he agreed.

The Doctor walked over to the body lying on its wheeled bed, and Henry lifted the sheet to disclose the bandaged head.

The two men peered at it intently.

"Isn't it amazing, Henry," whispered the Doctor, "that lying here within this skull is an artificially developed human brain; each cell, each convolution ready . . . waiting for the life to come. . . ."

He broke off as a clap of thunder drowned his speech.

"Look," he said, pointing through the window, "the storm is coming up over the mountains . . . it will soon be here."

Henry looked up towards the ceiling-trap, which was now closed.

"The kites . . . are they ready?"

Pretorius nodded.

"Yes," he said, turning and leaving the room.

"Then, said Henry to Franz, "send them up as soon as the wind rises. Hurry . . . hurry!"

The dwarf cupped his hand to his mouth, and bellowed:

"The kites . . . the kites . . . get 'em ready."

He walked over to the flight of stairs which led from the laboratory to the roof.

"I'll go up, sir and see that everything's in order."

"Yes," said Henry, "do. . . ."

The door opened, and the Doctor came in.

"Henry, you'll want some help. Where's Franz?"

"On the roof, seeing to the kites."

"Excellent! Now, let's see. . . ."

He walked over to the recumbent figure, Henry following. He lifted the cloth, and gazed intently at the bandaged face.

"Will it work, do you think?"

Henry sighed, shaking his head.

"Let us hope so," he murmured.

Above they could hear Franz shouting orders to the two men. The storm was very near now, and the lightning flashes were frequent and vivid.

The two men wheeled the bed over to the movable platform in the centre of the room, bolting the legs to the floor by means of ring shackles.

"The diffuser," said Henry.

The Doctor pulled the lever, and the diffuser in its cradle swung outward from the wall, until it was directly over the head of the figure. From its end hung two metal plates, not unlike a pair of cymbals, joined by a flexible arc of metal.

These plates Henry clamped against the ears of the figure. He walked over to a switchboard, consulted a row of gauges, and pressed down half-a-dozen switches.

Instantly, the low hum of released power sounded through the room. The floor trembled, and sparks coruscated at the terminals of the great condensers.

"Stand back!" Henry ordered, his hand on the master-switch.

CHAPTER XXV

THE TRIUMPH .

AT the top of the tower, two men were working by the light of flares, which danced and showered sparks in the wind. As they saw to the windlasses controlling the kites, the floor opened, and from below the Baron's voice shouted up:

"Stand by the roof!"

One of the men grasped a lever, and pulled it. Instantly the roof opened completely, disclosing the whole room beneath. They saw Henry turn the huge wheel that controlled the diffuser, adjusting it at the precise distance above the body.

"Now, men! Throw down the wires!"

The wires were rapidly unreeled, and Franz and Henry caught them as they fell, attaching them to the terminals on the head plates.

Henry looked up.

"All right! Stop the windlasses! I'm coming up!"

He ran lightly up the stairs, and came out upon the platform. He saw Franz and the Doctor standing by the body, and he waved to them.

He turned to his two assistants.

"Now . . . up with the kites! Did you snap the connections?"

"Yes, sir!"

"Stand by, then! Let go, Number One!"

The pawl was released on the ratchet wheel, and with a whine the windlass spun round as it paid out the rope. The wind caught the kite and swept it up at a giddy speed.

"Mind the handle," Henry warned. "Now, Number Two!"

The second kite followed, joining its companion far above the tower.

"Don't pay out the full length," Henry said. "I leave the kites to you."

He turned and ran down the stairs into the laboratory. He walked rapidly across to the circuit breaker, holding the switch in readiness against too great a current.

Above, the thunder was deafening, and his dials told him that the current passing through the condensers was terrific.

Lights flashed all around: great glass bulbs glowed and the arcs hissed between the dazzling white carbons.

And all the time the power was mounting: the great batteries were drinking in the tremendous flood of force; the needles were quivering on the dials at maximum pressure; and the whole tower shook with the stored-up potentiality of a force that could shatter a city.

Henry looked across at Pretorius, who was waiting, white and tense, by a lever.

He looked at the dials, and their quivering needles. The moment had come!

He waved his hand, too excited to speak: and Pretorius pushed the lever over.

Contact was made.

The diffuser hummed to the rush of power. The sparks leaped between its porcelain spheres, and a blue light played over their polished surfaces.

The great glass bulb glowed with a green light, flickering madly, and the transformers whined under a pressure mounting rapidly to the fantastic strength of a million volts.

Still Henry waited, watching the dials. The stupendous power was now passing through the recumbent body: too powerful to burn it. And for two hours, the lights played about the strange instruments, and the laboratory hummed with the caged power of the elemental force.

Then at last, Henry decided that the moment had come for cosmic power to be used.

He shut off the circuit-breaker, yelling through the open shaft to the men above.

"Ready . . . it's coming up!"

The two men above, looking down, saw Henry pull the contact-lever; then pull the other lever, which set the mechanism of the diffuser in motion.

As they watched, the table rose, with the body on it. There were explosions, sparks, puffs of smoke. The table rose higher and higher; the sparks pouring out of the diffuser suspended over the body.

From below, Henry and the Doctor watched the ascending mechanism.

The electrical discharge from the cables of the kites was constant, and the flashes were now almost continuous.

On the roof, the men also were gazing upwards. One man went below, and the other remained on guard.

But so intent was he in watching the rising table, that he did not see a tall gaunt shape that came shuffling up the stairs, gazing in childish curiosity about him.

Then the man saw him, and yelled:

"Get down from here! Get down!"

The Monster stood still, growling.

"I told you to get away! Get away! Get away!"

The man cast a terrified glance at the diffuser. What would happen if the Monster interfered *now,* he dared not think.

Frightened almost out of his wits, the fellow screamed:

"Get away! Get away!"

He grabbed a torch from its holder, and turned towards the Monster, with the intention of scaring him away. But the fire revived memories in the dull mind, and in a second the gaunt shape had hurled itself at the man. There was a struggle; the torch fell, and was picked up by the Monster, who struck at the fallen man with the flaming wood.

Then he picked up the man, and threw him over the parapet.

As he went screaming down to death, the Monster screamed in sympathy.

Then cautiously he went over to the opening, and peered down into the room below.

He heard Henry say:

"That's enough," and saw his hand move a lever. Instantly the table began to ascend.

A fire-ball met the diffuser, and broke in a shower of sparks. The Monster dodged the fiery rain, and ran, panting and frightened, to the shelter of the parapet.

As the table came to rest on the floor of the laboratory, Henry ordered:

"Ready to take off the diffuser!"

Franz and the Doctor moved over towards the table.

"Remove the diffuser plates."

The Doctor unclamped the cymbal-like plates, and while Franz grasped one of the figure's hands, Pretorius grasped the other.

Their eyes met across the bandaged body: in the Doctor's was triumph: in Franz's something not so easily analysed.

Henry bent over the figure, and removed the bandage from its eyes.

For a long second he stood motionless, gazing down at those clear blue eyes.

Then he whispered:

"She's alive! . . . Alive. . . !"

Pretorius nodded, and signed to Franz. Grasping the table-top, they tipped it forward, thus bringing the body to an upright position.

So the three of them stood, staring at the bandaged figure . . . and those limped eyes.

Then, as they watched, the arms began to move . . . to lift . . . while the staring, yet uncomprehending eyes, moved jerkily from side to side.

Pretorius gazed in rapture at the moving arms: then at Henry: then back in a sort of gloating hysterical triumph, to the girl.

Now suddenly the arms dropped; and as if exhausted by these pre-liminary manifestations of newly-awakened life, the head fell forward on the figure's breast.

Henry jumped and held the head up, while Pretorius unwound the bandages that covered all the face but the eyes.

And as they unwound the cerement-like wrappings, so their wonder grew.

For the flesh that lay revealed beneath, the smooth firm contours of a young girl's face, was flushed with the bloom of youthful health.

With active fingers the Doctor removed the other bandages that en-wrapped the body. There was a curious brown pigmentation on the inside aspect of the right thigh, but apart from that, the skin (except of course, for the scarlet lines of the scars) was smooth and white.

She stood upright, like a lay figure, while the Doctor and Henry stepped back to examine in awesome silence their handiwork.

"She is . . . beautiful," the Doctor whispered after a while.

"Yes . . . she is beautiful. . . !"

Above that small face, with its wide, staring eyes, the hair grew strangely straight and long. It radiated fan-wise from her brow, like some outlandish head-dress, and on the left side, a white streak showed vividly against the raven black of the rest.

"Faulty pigmentation again," the Doctor muttered.

But Henry said nothing: he was to rapt in the contemplation of this lovely alien thing.

So quietly she stood there: so lovely, and unashamed, in all her white beauty. . . !

The eyes were fixed on his, and as he watched, the curved lips pouted.

Her head turned jerkily from side to side: her arms rose slowly, as before; and her delicate foot took a step forward.

When she had taken half-a-dozen steps, she swayed; and had not the Doctor been watching her intently, she would have fallen.

With Henry holding one hand, and he the other, they led her slowly across the room.

"She must learn to walk first," said the Doctor. "It is not weakness so much, as want of practice."

Slowly, one step at a time, they led her down the length of the big room. Then, at the farther wall, they sat her down in a chair, while they stood examining her face for signs of fatigue.

So immersed were they, indeed, that they did not hear the door open behind them, and a gaunt shape, as horrible as this was lovely, pad silently into the room.

They were only aware of the intrusions as, in hateful, familiar tones, the cry: "Friend . . . !" fell upon their startled ears, and the eyes before them filled with emotion for the first time; the emotion of *fear*. . . .

Pretorius and Henry turned round to confront the Monster; but his regard was not for them.

Grinning foolishly, he stumbled towards the seated girl, his hands working spasmodically, with the pleasurable excitement that was filling him.

"Friend . . ." he mouthed, drooling with obscene desire, ". . . friend . . . !"

And now life came swift and sudden to the seated figure. The grinning face was very near her own, when she screamed. Stridently: frenzied. Screamed again, and again, and again; until with a gasp, she fell forward, and Henry caught her in his arms.

Tenderly he bore her to the sofa and laid her down. The Monster came ambling behind him, hands and eyes twitching with nervous excitement.

He put out a hand to caress the recumbent girl: but the Doctor pulled him roughly aside.

"Stand back!" he snarled.

The Monster paid no attention. He brushed the Doctor aside, and sat down on the sofa, taking the girl's hand and fondling it with clumsy endearments.

"Oh God! Henry, what *are* we to do?"

He turned angrily to the Monster.

"Stand back, you!"

Henry whispered:

"Wait. . . ."

The girl was beginning now to recover. An eyelid flickered, and her breathing became regular. The Monster was still chafing her hand.

Her eyes opened, and she saw the dreadful face beside her.

Her hand drew back in terror.

"Wait . . ." said Henry.

The Monster put his paw on her white thigh; stroking the soft, smooth skin.

"Friend. . . ."

There was a scream: this time almost more penetrating than before. The girl jumped up from the sofa, and ran to Henry.

He put his arms about her, contemptuous of the Monster's snarls.

"Listen, Pretorius, I'm taking her downstairs. I'll wrap her up, and give her some food." He looked disdainfully at the Monster, as he added, "See if you can keep this *thing* quiet!"

As the door closed behind them, the Monster growled:

"She hates me . . . like others. . . ."

"No . . . no," the Doctor said soothingly. "She is tired."

The Monster seemed to consider that. He blinked suspiciously at the Doctor, then gazed uncertainly at the closed door.

He shook his head.

"No . . . ." he said deliberately, "she hates me . . . like others. . . ."

And then a slow, evil smile passed across that white scarred face: and seeing it, the Doctor's soul sickened within him.

The Monster nodded.

"You make . . . her?" pointing with a long dirty finger at the other.

"Yes!" Pretorius whispered, through dry lips.

The Monster nodded.

"Then . . . she . . . belongs . . . me?" he leered, and turned towards the door.

Perhaps, in some awful moment, Dr. Pretorius found his sanity. Perhaps, as the Monster moved off, he realized what a terrible price one must pay when one tampers with those things that a Divine Wisdom has bidden us to leave alone.

In one sickening flash of understanding, he realized that what had been created a slave, was now their master. That the destiny of all of them was in the hands, and at the whim, of this ungainly, uncomely, half-witted brute.

For never an impulse that would come to him would go unsatisfied. Neither reason, nor propriety, not pity, nor shame, would defeat his purpose. He was something lower than lowest creation: and yet in his elemental *singleness* of purpose, in this utter contempt of any other consideration but the immediate satisfying of his desires, he was greater than them all.

It was with this realization that the Doctor flung himself across the room, just as the Monster's hand was on the handle of the door.

The Monster turned, snarling.

"No!"

Pretorius struck at him with his weakened, yet still active strength.

The Monster growled menacingly.

"Come back," the Doctor yelled, pulling at the collar of the Monster's coat.

A heavy fist was raised, and the Doctor staggered back, the blood pouring from his smashed mouth

"Go away!" the Monster muttered, and opened the door.

CHAPTER XXVI

FINALE

THE Doctor heard his heavy footsteps on the wooden stairs: but for a few moments he could do nothing but lie where he had fallen. He pulled a handkerchief from his pocket, and dabbed tenderly at his rapidly-swelling lips.

Then he stumbled to his feet and, going over to the small sink in the corner of the laboratory, rinsed his mouth, spitting out two teeth with a wry smile. The Doctor had not yet lost his sense of humour.

Then from below came a cry of alarm. Instantly the Doctor raced across the room, and ran down the stairs.

It was as he had thought. . . .

The Monster was standing just inside the door, gazing at the girl, around whom Henry's protecting arms were encircled.

For one second the tableau stood. Then with a low growl the Monster began to move towards the girl.

Henry, catching sight of Pretorius's white face beyond the door, yelled: "Doctor, stop him, for God's sake!"

The Doctor rushed into the room and, with a deft movement, thrust a long, wheeled operating-table between the Monster and the girl. Baffled, the gaunt figure gazed at the Doctor in bewilderment. He moved to the side, and the Doctor manœuvred the table around him.

"Henry," he panted, "get her out of this, while I play him. . . ."

He kept the table moving, while Henry edged the girl in the direction of the door.

But the Monster, for all his dull wits, had not missed the significance of the manœuvre. Thwarted desire had lent wings to his imagination.

With a snarling cry, he caught the table with both hands, and, exerting his tremendous strength, sent it hurtling across the room.

The girl screamed, and Henry's face paled, as he saw the last obstacle go. Pretorius rushed between them and the Monster, clawing desperately at his twitching face.

The great hands beat down on the Doctor's grey head, but the desperate hold did not relax.

Then, with a mighty blow, the Doctor was flung to the ground, just as the Monster staggered up to the great lever which controlled the electrical power.

A hoarse cry broke from Henry, as he saw that the Monster's waving arm was perilously near to the lever.

"Look out! Pretorius, the lever!"

From the ground, the Doctor saw and shuddered.

"The lever!" He scrambled to his feet, and walked across to where the Monster stood, blinking suspiciously. He pointed to the switch with a trembling hand.

"The lever . . . look out for that lever! You'll blow us all to atoms. . . !"

Then came the most surprising thing of all.

A voice called sharply through the grille of the outer door:

"Henry!"

There was a gasping cry:

"Elizabeth!"

They could see her white face through the little grille, as she beat on the ancient oak of the door.

"Open the door! Quick!"

Henry, his arms around the girl, shouted, terrified:

"Get back! Get back!"

She was clinging to the bars, hysterical, as she screamed:

"I won't unless you come!"

Then, putting the girl aside, Henry rushed to the door, sliding back the rusty bolts.

"My darling!" Henry murmured brokenly, "you must go. I can't leave them . . . I can't!"

But now another voice spoke: and this time, with a strange authority.

"Go!" said the Monster. His hand was on the lever.

Henry saw, and thrust Elizabeth out into the night. She was determined not to go without him: and he was equally determined to stay.

The harsh voice behind them said:

"They stay . . . we belong . . . dead."

His fingers were trembling on the lever, as he grinned at the Doctor.

"No . . .no!" Pretorius's voice was a choking sob; and he began to sidle towards the door.

Then through the room came a shape in headlong flight.

Strong arms pushed Henry and Elizabeth through the doorway on to the stone ramp that ran down to the heath.

"Run, you weak fool," Franz cried.

He turned in the doorway as the Doctor hurled himself through. His muscular arms caught the rushing figure and flung it back.

"My triumph, Doctor! Go back to your magical instruments . . . *cheat!*"

He pulled the door to, and thrust a key into the lock.

Through the open grille he could see the Doctor's white face, as he screamed for mercy.

But there was no time to gloat.

He flung the key away and raced down the ramp. Henry and Elizabeth were still running, when they heard the girl's wild scream and the Doctor's despairing cry.

Then it seemed as though the artillery of God had thundered forth. There was a dull, monstrous roar, and a blinding flash. A rush of wind that threw them to the ground: the crash of falling masonry: and a cloud across the setting moon.

As in a trance, they stood gazing at the mound that was the grave of much more than three bodies.

A voice said:

"Gaze long, Baron: for you will never see its like again!"

Elizabeth murmured:

"Franz, we owe you a debt of gratitude. . . ."

The dwarf smiled wistfully.

"You were kind to me," he said simply, "though I did you a wrong."

They stood there a while in silence, revolving many memories; until at last the hunchback said:

"Good-bye . . . it will soon be dawn. . . ."

"Good-bye, my friend . . . ." said Henry. And turning to Elizabeth he whispered "Our dawn!" as he folded her in his arms.

THE END

153